SKYLARKING

KATE MILDENHALL

Legend Press Ltd, 107-111 Fleet Street, London, EC4A 2AB
info@legend-paperbooks.co.uk | www.legendpress.co.uk

Contents © Kate Mildenhall 2016

First published by Black Inc., an imprint of Schwartz Publishing Pty Ltd,
Level 1, 221 Drummond Street, Carlton VIC 3053, Australia
www.blackincbooks.com

Print ISBN 978-1-7850792-3-8
Ebook ISBN 978-1-7850792-2-1
Set in Times. Printed by Opolgraf SA.
Cover design by Gudrun Jobst www.yotedesign.com

Kate Mildenhall is a writer and education project officer, who currently works at the State Library of Victoria. As a teacher, she has worked in schools, at RMIT University and has volunteered with Teachers Across Borders in Cambodia.

Skylarking is her debut novel. She discovered the story while on a camping trip and she wishes for more such fruitful adventures. She lives with her husband and two young daughters in Hurstbridge, Victoria.

Visit Kate at
katemildenhall.com
Or on Twitter
@katemildenhall

To Gracie and Etta,
may you know friendship, as I have,
in all its ferocity and wonder

PROLOGUE

The sky was clear and blue forever that day. Clear and blue and so bright. Sunlight fell through the leaves, forming dark shadows and spots so blindingly white they forced me to look away. Harriet had packed a picnic: some ginger cake, half a loaf of soda bread, a square of butter wrapped in waxed paper. It seemed the beginning of something, this day – the sun, our being together again, making our way down the track to McPhail's hut.

I remember our chatter. I remember her grip on my wrist. I remember her veering from the track, pointing towards the hut, the absence of smoke from the chimney. I remember the empty echo of our knocks on the door. I remember letting ourselves in. I remember the hat, and the voice I used, strange and deep, that I pulled from somewhere inside me to make her laugh. Always, always, to make her laugh.

I remember the way Harriet turned, breathless, laughing, a strand of her golden hair caught on her bottom lip.

After that, I try not to remember.

ONE

They chose a good spot for our lighthouse. High on the layered stone of a cliff face that jutted out, decisively, into the ocean; it was the kind of location that seemed confident, arrogant enough for a lighthouse. The dusty scrub of the headland stood hardly as high as the height of a man. While the sky was often endless and vivid, as soon as you left the grassy green slope of the lighthouse paddock, you could feel trapped and airless in the twiggy underbrush of the ti-tree and the thick canopy that blocked out the sky and muffled the sound of the waves. From the edge of the cliff, or as close to the edge as I had ever dared to go, there was only ocean and ocean and ocean, stretched out in the silky blue of a lady's skirt, all the way to the horizon.

I was nine, Harriet eleven, when we first clambered out over the stone wall to stand on the farthest point. It was one of those days where the sun glare made my eyes ache, and the sky was clear in a great arc, but the wind off the sea whipped any heat out of the day and forced watery tears down my cheeks. We had already taken our turn at dragging the bedding into the laundry in great piles and heaving the sodden mass out again to be thrashed dry by the nor'westerly. Now we were free.

We knew the rules about the wall and the cliffs, and the warnings we'd been told since we were small about how easily we could tumble over the cliff's edge and be dashed upon the rocks below, or swallowed up by the waves or, worse still, gnashed in the jaws of a great white shark. As a child, the threat of what lay beyond that wall was enough for me. Sitting in the latrine that had been built high out on a ledge over the sea, I could look down between my legs and see the foaming white froth spill over the rocks far beneath me. I would swallow hard and feel a roar in my ears until I could fix my gaze upon the swinging wooden door.

So I had kept away from the cliff. But now Harriet and I thought we were the oldest and wisest young ladies of the colony. What Harriet had in her two years of seniority to me, I made up for in bravery and cheek. You couldn't have picked it then; it was only later, when it was obvious Harriet was becoming a young woman and I was yet to outgrow my childhood body, that you'd have said she was clearly the eldest.

'Bet you'll never go beyond the wall,' I said to Harriet as we lay on the grass.

'Probably not.' Harriet was a lazy type of beautiful, sweet and curly and far too used to being mollycoddled by her mother. She didn't see the point in doing anything outlandish; she didn't feel the fire as I had begun to. At least, she didn't feel it then.

'I would do it.'

'No, you wouldn't, you just say that. You've a big mouth, Kate Gilbert, but you're not as brave as you think.'

A blush burned up my cheeks. I hated that I was laid bare before her.

'I'll tell you what the view is like when I get back.' I scrambled up and stomped towards the lighthouse and the stone wall that lay beyond.

'Kate, I didn't mean it. Please don't. Your mother will be livid.'

'I don't care,' I called over my shoulder into the wind.

I knew she would chase after me – she always did. By the time I was at the low rock wall, she was beside me, breathing hard.

'Come on, Harriet! I won't fall if you hold my hand,' I said as I stepped over.

She glared at me but hooked her leg over the low wall and followed me through the prickly heath towards the edge. Only that few feet closer to the sea, and the sound was magnified, a crashing thud that echoed up through the solid rock and vibrated in my body and my ears. I was consumed by it. It was as though a single thread had been plucked from my dress and stretched all the way to the cottage where Mother would be bustling about in the kitchen. It held me, but it was thin, and it blew out in an arc like a spider's silk in the wind. I reached for Harriet's hand and told her where to place her black boots as we inched forwards in the shifting stones.

I was a lighthouse girl and I had stood on the edge of cliffs before, but not this one, and never so high up. Harriet stopped and let go of my hand as we got closer, spooked by the buffeting wind and the sudden space that was opening up before us where the edge of the rock dropped into nothingness.

'Kate, this is far enough. We've seen it; we've gone further out than the boys. It could crumble away.' Harriet was frozen, white hands gripping a salt bush that would do nothing to hold her if she slipped.

'I want to see over the edge,' I shouted, and my mouth filled with cold air as the sound was snatched away from me.

'Well, I'm not going any further. You'll get yourself killed!'

I turned. 'Come with me, Harriet, just a little bit further. I won't let you fall.'

Her face was white and creased with worry. Some part of me, deep inside, grew stronger when Harriet was scared. I needed her beside me, to feel her trembling hand in mine, to have the courage to get to the edge myself. I took her hand.

'We'll go slowly; you tell me if you need to stop. Just to that rock there. We'll be able to see the whole world.' Her face did not shift, but she began to move her feet. Together we crept forwards, bodies braced against the wind, the sea glittering in front of us and all around.

'Kate …' Harriet warned me, and I knew it was close enough.

Below us the rocks looked as if they had crumbled into the sea. To the right there was a river of brown and green glinting in the sunlight, broken glass where the men tipped our rubbish over the edge. Out beyond the swirls of white water and dark shadows of submerged rock, birds circled and then plunged into the water, leaving small splashes in their wake. The silvery glint of a school of fish flashed under the surface of the water. The sound of the wind out there was a high whistle in my ears, and I clapped my other hand up to stop the cold prick of it worming into my brain.

'Oh,' breathed Harriet, her face close to my ear.

I turned to see her eyes bright with the light and the water and the brilliance of it all.

This was surely joy. And terror – for I was seized by the thought, so clear, that I could step forwards and then be falling, weightless. And more than that: Harriet's trust was so warm and damp in the grip of my hand; I could take her with me. We could be like sisters forever, leaping out into the air. Perhaps we would find that we could fly, and we would circle up and up, calling to each other, laughing at the wonder of it, looking down at the lighthouse, the cottages, the slope of green speckled with goats, the little paths etched through the scrub, the shapes of the children playing, as we circled ever higher, unbound by the earth.

I stepped back suddenly, pulling Harriet with me, and sat down with a thud.

'Kate! You scared me!' Harriet crouched down next to me. 'You're as white as a ghost.'

'I was dizzy, that's all.' My head spun, and the sun was dazzling.

'Come on,' she said and heaved me up and back towards

the solid bulk of the lighthouse, the settlement, all our earthly goods.

I still see it sometimes, in my dreams, my mind's eye. I see it but not quite as it was, and I wonder what other imaginings I have mixed up with the truth of the past. The two of us, arms outstretched to the sky, the sea, fingertips touching, and the wind rushing through us, our hair, our skirts, our breathless laughter as we stood on the edge of terror and wonder and marvelled at how brave we were.

TWO

I don't remember life before Harriet.

History will tell that there was a point in time when I was just Kate, and Harriet just Harriet. But everyone on the cape understands that from the day she arrived we became Kate and Harriet. Harriet and Kate. One did not fully exist without the other. The story goes that we ran towards each other, Harriet some weeks past her fifth birthday and me just shy of my third, and clapped hands in delight at the sight of the other. From then on we shared everything. Games and dolls and secrets and adventures and, once we grew older, the chores and then school that filled our mornings before we were released to run wild upon our cape. Not sisters, but we might as well have been. At some point I realised that it was mere chance that Harriet and I had been put on this earth at the same time, on the same stretch of land. It made me fearful. For if God held such power, the power to make me so infinitely complete, could he not also hold the power to make me the opposite?

Harriet loved me like a sister because she had no siblings. Only later would I truly know what it must have been like for Mrs Walker, Harriet's mother, to have lost her second child before its time and then to lose that very bit of her that could ever bear a child again. I, on the other hand, soon had a sister, Emmaline, four years my junior whom Harriet and I delighted in cuddling, but whom we grew tired of once she reached the age where she could talk. I tried to get our brothers to play with her instead – James, who was one year older than Emmaline, and William, who arrived two years after her; but the boys stuck together, as they do, and Emmaline was always somewhat on the outer. I felt guilty for it sometimes. But not enough to let her in. After Harriet, my brother George had been my favourite but he had gone and died of pleurisy and left me eldest. At nine, I still found it hard to decide if I was angry at him for this fact or only sad.

I was dark, and Harriet was fair. I, loud; she, prim. Harriet of the golden curls. Harriet, who seemed to absorb light and burnish it and throw it back out through her hair and her skin and her eyes so that to be in her presence was to be bathed in it. When visitors came to the cape they would gasp and put their hands out to touch Harriet, as though it were incredible to find such a glowing, radiant being on this ragged bit of coast. She collected ribbons, and I coveted books.

I remember the day my most-treasured book arrived aboard the supply boat by way of a parcel from Harriet's aunt. Harriet and I were bursting with anticipation when we saw the post amongst the supplies waiting to be delivered and ferried up the track to the station. The supply boat only got to us every two months so there were always plenty of packages and sacks and boxes to be unloaded. After we had run back and forth distributing tea here and sugar there and fresh meat and butter, and the store cupboards of each of the cottages were again stocked with goods, Harriet and I raced to her room with the parcel and shut the door.

We sat atop Harriet's bed with our legs crossed, the package between us. It was heavy and rectangular, wrapped tightly in brown paper and tied with string. Sometimes her aunt would include a satin ribbon, or a tin of sweet biscuits, once four tubes of paint – red, blue, yellow and white – and a beautiful wooden brush. My fingers itched to rip at the paper and have the contents revealed in all their glory, but Harriet preferred to go slowly, savour the moment, and it was, after all, addressed to her. Harriet unknotted the string while I wriggled impatiently.

'Go on, then. You do the paper,' she said and passed the package to me.

I was careful not to tear it; we would use every inch of that paper for drawing and painting later. Finally the contents lay before us. Two magazines, a pair of red woollen socks, a small book of nursery rhymes and a larger parcel, with a message in cursive on a card fixed to the top.

On the occasion of your twelfth birthday, dear Harriet. May you derive your own valuable information, pleasure, great profit and unbounded amusement from these pages.

Harriet picked up the package and weighed it in her hands. 'It's another book,' she said, rolling her eyes.

Her aunt, Cecilia Butterworth, was both appalled and thrilled by the notion of her brother raising his only child on an outpost such as our cape. She saw it as her duty to take charge of Harriet's cultural education. She did not, of course, know that Harriet never read the books she was sent, for I begged Harriet not to say, and instead I devoured each one as it arrived, and then again, many times thereafter.

Harriet passed this smaller parcel to me and threw herself back on her pillow with one of the magazines.

I held it reverently in my hands and eased the wrapping back. A book thick with many pages and a soft leather cover in green with a title inlaid in the centre: *The Coral Island.*

I must have had some inkling then of what those pages would give me, of what pictures and ideas would be imprinted on my mind forever more, for it was as though I could hear a whooshing sound, like that when Father lit the lamp, the sound right before it began to glow, getting louder and brighter as it went.

Poor Harriet lost me for a few days after that. She would

appear on our verandah, her face wide open and ready for whatever adventure the day might present; I would only raise my head from the book, shake it and go back to the brilliant blue waters and soft breezes of the Pacific, and the adventures of Ralph and Jack and Peterkin.

I wondered at the preface to the book many times. The words impressed a certain pattern on my mind and the back of my tongue, and I felt them thudding softly there as my eyes flitted across the page.

…If there is a boy or man who loves to be melancholy and morose, and who cannot enter with kindly sympathy into the regions of fun, let me seriously advise him to shut my book and put it away. It is not meant for him.

And by omission, not meant for me. For girls, or women, or any of our sex at all. Despite the closed door of this first page that tried to hold me back from the adventures within, I rushed on headfirst into a world of deserted beaches, and dark savages made good and kind by the lightness of God, the paradise of friendship and camaraderie in the face of adversity. Reading it made me feel as though I, too, were part of some grand tradition.

The only problem was, of course, that I wasn't going anywhere. Being the daughter of the head lighthouse keeper on a remote cape in a young colony was an adventure of sorts, I supposed. But I watched the ships sail by from the cliff top and knew that they would not stop for me.

On fine days, I sat out on the orange rock that was shaped like a steamed pudding and imagined how Harriet and I might sail off together. Even though the peppery scent of the scrub on that headland ran through my blood, I knew that there must be other places that would thrill me. And while I hoped that Harriet would be by my side as I adventured off into the great unknown, I knew this was unlikely. Where I had dreams of boats and pirates and coral island adventures, Harriet saw a future of a home and hearth filled with all the babies her mother had failed to have.

I never dreamed that it would be Harriet who left before I did.

THREE

The post that arrived for Father told another story.

'So, they're finally sending me a second assistant,' he said to Mother over the top of the letter as I set his cup of tea in front of him.

Mother paused drying a plate. 'A single man, or a family?'

'A family by the looks, a growing one at that.'

'Are there children?' I asked, leaning in over his shoulder so that I might read the letter, too, but he shifted it from the light.

'A Mr Ernest Jackson and his young wife Mary, with a new baby girl.'

I supposed a baby would be nice enough, a little one to fuss over. But it was someone our age, Harriet's or mine, who I really wanted. Either to love or loathe, I didn't mind which. As long as they brought tales of somewhere else and allowed themselves to be examined by Harriet and me, the way a naturalist might examine a new species so that they might learn something of the world, then they would be welcome.

'There's some older children, too. A boy of nine, from another wife, now dead, and a younger boy.'

'Playmates for all of you then. Your brothers and Emmaline will be pleased,' Mother said. 'When are they expected?'

'By the end of the month, it says. We'll finally have someone to fill the last cottage.'

'It'll be needing a good clean before they arrive. Sounds

like Mrs Jackson will have her hands full when she gets here. Where do you think you're going, young lady?'

I stopped halfway to the door. 'Do let me go and tell Harriet the news before bed. I won't be long.'

'It can wait till the morning. Honestly, you have all the time in the world to share your news and your stories. You're not going anywhere. Help me with these and then we'll get the children ready for a wash.'

Father got up and placed his hand on my shoulder as he made for the door and his shift on the light. 'If you get your chores done, you can bring me up my cup of tea before you turn in for the night,' he said.

I nodded – there was that, at least.

Ever since we had been able to climb the one hundred and sixty-two steps of the lighthouse, it had been a magical place for Harriet and me. If the day was clear and our fathers were jolly enough to let us play on their hallowed ground, we imagined ourselves rulers of all we could see. Because I was dark-haired where Harriet was blonde, it fell to me to play the king or the prince while she was the queen or else the fair maiden trapped by a wicked witch in the tower. We might pretend to make ourselves useful polishing the brass, or sweeping the many iron steps, but all the while we spoke in the riddles of our imagined world. When we could convince them, we would tempt one of the younger children to the tower with promises of wondrous sights or cake, and then we would hold them captive until they begged for our mercy.

I learned later that my father, while pedantic about all things to do with his lighthouse keeping, was relatively relaxed when it came to the rules of the settlement. I never knew any other way than being permitted to cavort in the lighthouse, to run and play in Harriet's cottage or she in mine when we desired, but the stories that came to us of other light stations were often of unbending hierarchy: children only allowed to play together in common areas outside and sometimes not at all. I couldn't imagine how those families didn't go mad under the strict rule of a head keeper so unyielding. We had no such problem on our cape.

Sometimes our fathers let us sit in the light, or perch on the narrow ledge that circled the inside of the glass. If there was no gale, we could go through the door and out onto the high-railed balcony that ran around the top of the tower. We would stand with our backs pressed against the whitewashed stone, the wind whipping hair across our faces and stealing the breath from our lips, and peer down at the skeleton of the *SS Hamilton* submerged in the waves below.

I had not been alive when it was wrecked, but I knew the stories of the stormy night, the calls for help, so like the calling of seals that they were not noticed at first. Most of the crew had been rescued, although the captain, refusing to move until every last man was off the ship, had been swept off the mast he was clinging to by an enormous wave.

My father was patient with our presence in the lighthouse. But a lighthouse keeper has to be a patient man. The never-ending polishing, lighting, staring out to sea, one's whole body tuned for disaster, would send many men mad. But my father could polish that glass until the light fairly cut from it, a blade in the night sky, warning the seafarers. There is honour in lighthouse keeping. I would go to bed each night knowing that my father – or Harriet's father, Walker, who was the first assistant – were watching over us. And protecting more than simply our families at the light station, but also the countless passengers, sailors, captains and fishermen who sailed past our little jut of coast, casting their eyes out into the dark for the steady beam, the signature of our light. Blink, flash, blink.

While I loved the games Harriet and I played in the lighthouse, I also loved nights like this one, where I could visit Father high in the tower, and it was only him and me.

'Father, did you always want to be a lighthouse keeper?' I often asked.

'For as long as I can remember,' he would reply.

'But why?'

And even though I asked him countless times, he would always stop and stroke his chin and come up with a different answer. For the safety of those at sea, he might say, or to keep an eye on the fish. To get your mother out of the city, was another answer he might give, even though I knew full well that my mother needed much convincing when her sweetheart had revealed his intention, and that this was another story altogether.

Father lit the lamp by gently pumping the kerosene into the lantern. Every time, I was thrilled by the whooshing sound and the glow that followed. With the lamp lit, attention moved to keeping the great glass lantern turning. Father let me place my hands on the lever and he would close his great big hands over mine and together we would turn, feeling the drag of the weights on the wires that were funnelled down the stone core of the lighthouse.

I put the thermos of tea on his small desk.

'You're looking at your maps again,' I said.

'Indeed.'

Father loved maps. He liked to tell me how many he had. Maps of the coast, of the ocean, of the mountains that ran like a seam and had blocked all attempts at finding the great inland sea. Long rolls of thick paper covered in lines and curves and strange markings, impossible for a young girl to understand. It was a lighthouse keeper's duty, Father would say, to know the lie of the land and the signs of the sea. And so he would pore over his collection, memorising the details. I thought once that he must dream of his own adventures; but I know now he was simply transfixed by understanding every inch of the land around us. There were jagged lines that appeared to mark the space between land and water, and star-shaped compass points to tell the place on the globe.

I leaned in towards the maps that were unrolled on his desk that night as though they were a magnet and I a little tack.

'What do they say, Father?'

'You ask so many questions, Kate – one day you'll stump me.'

'What's this bit?' I pointed my index finger at rings of crinkled lines; in and out they went in tighter and tighter circles.

'Contour lines – those are mountains. The lines tell you how high and steep they are.'

'But I can't tell they're mountains. How do you know?'

'It's like a language, a language of maps. I know the language so I can read the map.'

'I want to learn the language, too.'

'Well, one day you might, my dearest, one day you might.'

Father rolled up the maps and that was that. But I thought about them. Thought about how little they told of the places they meant to represent. How can someone look at a map and understand the ache of a steep climb, the crick in the neck of looking up through tangled trees to see the ridgeline and the sky blown wide open above it? How can one know a mountain unless they have stood upon the highest point and understood how it sits amongst the other peaks and valleys, known the shape of the land around it? Those maps were a poor attempt to replicate a mountain but, I came to realise, a useful one all the same.

What I understood as I grew was that the maps didn't tell the whole story. Sometimes they even told the wrong story, their infinitesimal errors meaning men were lost in deserts, ships speared upon rocky reefs, land taken up when it belonged to someone else.

I had once tried showing Harriet the maps, tried explaining their strange beauty that had so entranced me. But she did not care for them. Well, she liked to know which direction Melbourne was, and that to get to Sydney one travelled the opposite way and for a number of days longer. But she became sulky when I spent too long with them.

'Are you plotting your escape then?' she would ask. 'Is that why you spend so long on them?

22

No, and yes. How could I explain that to see our cape rendered there on the map, defined in its space, made me want to travel both far from it and, at the same time, never leave? How could I want one thing so much and its exact opposite at the same time?

'Time for bed then, Kate,' Father said, and I gathered up the tea things.

'I'm glad you'll have your new assistant, Father.'

'As am I. We'll have a chance to get things fixed up around the place, and Walker and I won't be spread so thin.'

''Night then, Father.'

He kissed me on the top of the head, and I rattled back down the steps, thinking about maps and journeys. Thinking that if I couldn't head off in my own little boat, then at least there was a new family arriving who might bring some adventure to me.

FOUR

The Jacksons arrived three weeks later. They came by boat, and we all traipsed down to the jetty to see them disembark. At first we thought that Mrs Jackson might not step foot on the jetty, so white was she. They'd travelled for days, overland from down near Ballarat and then the last part, from Edenstown, by boat. I couldn't be sure if it was an upset belly from the long journey or fear of what lay ahead that kept her there on the boat while her husband unloaded and shook Father's hand, as did the eldest boy, who had the air of someone old before his time.

I stepped forwards and thrust out my hand. 'I'm Kate.'

He was slow to respond but finally said, 'Albert.' A younger boy, with dark hair unlike his brother's, scampered up behind him. 'And this is Harold.'

'Harry,' the younger boy said, and grinned. 'My baby sister – she's called Lucy.'

I took his hand in mine, too. 'Welcome to the cape, Harry,' I said. 'Come on, this way.' I picked up one of the packages from the pile and went to lead up the path. I noticed Mrs Jackson, now on dry land with her baby bundled in blankets against her chest, narrow her gaze at me.

It would become clear over the coming weeks that Mrs Jackson was going to take some time to get used to the new etiquette of the cape, where girls like me could shoot out a hand to a boy and assume it would be shaken. In fact, she never warmed to me. It made things easier for her later, I suppose.

Harriet and I took it on as our duty to introduce the Jackson boys to the cape. Once we'd given them the tour of the lighthouse, the three cottages, the outhouse, water tanks and sheds, the yard for our goats and the small paddock for the three horses, there was no better way to show the rest than to make them play our favourite game – hide and seek – amongst the ti-tree that hunched against the sloping cliffs. Even then, aged ten and twelve, we had not outgrown the game of our childhood, and the younger children never needed to whine at us too long before we agreed to play, for it was a pleasure indeed to dip into that dense scrub and suddenly be hidden deep in its quiet, protected world.

On this afternoon, a blustery cold wind blew scudding messy clouds across the sky, every now and then revealing the sun. We gathered together at the edge of the ti-tree. I cleared my throat and spelled out the rules for the benefit of our newcomers. Someone must be seeker, to stand in one spot with eyes closed and count to one hundred, not too fast and not too slow, calling the numbers so that the hiders could hear them and not be ambushed before they had a chance to tuck themselves away. No giving away the spots of others. The first person found was seeker the next round; the last had the glory. The far boundary of the game was where the scrub tilted down into the crumbling cliff face – and no further.

On this day, I picked Harriet as seeker.

'That's not fair!' Emmaline cried, stamping her little foot and pouting. 'Harriet and you always go first!'

'That's not true, Emmaline,' I said, smiling sweetly and pulling her to my side, all the while pinching her under her arm, on the chubby soft flesh where it would hurt. 'We're the big girls, so we get to decide.'

'Ow!' she yelled. 'Albert's big, too. Now he should be in charge.'

'Not as big as us,' I said, putting an end to her whining. 'Let's start.'

Harriet began to count. Everyone ran helter-skelter for a spot. I loved the sound of quick breaths and twigs snapping underfoot, branches rubbing against each other as we scurried to find our places. I headed towards the furthermost part of the ti-tree, nearest the cliff edge. After a time, the only sounds were the murmurings of the little ones who couldn't stay silent in their hiding places.

I wiggled into a space, a tunnel formed in the understorey of the ti-tree. It was hushed and windless in there and, when I rested my head on my arm, I could lie back comfortably and see the way the light fell through the maze of branches and leaves. I was very quiet.

I watched a willy wagtail jumping up on a branch and down again, fanning its black and white tail from side to side, cocking its head at me inquisitively. The bird called, a high whistling tune, and then ducked and took off, finding an invisible, impossible path through the thick brush and disappearing from my view.

'Ninety-eight, ninety-nine, one hundred!'

I raised my head so I could peer through the trees at Harriet as she opened her eyes. She rubbed them, squinting into the bush, trying to make sense of the darkness there, the cross hatch of twigs and dead foliage and green. She smiled at the hushed sound of giggling coming from the cover of trees.

'Ready or not, I'm coming!' she called, and crept away from me towards the noise.

I listened to the sounds of the first ones being discovered, the squeals and the shouts. The rules were that as each hider was found, they joined the seeker and became a roving pack, blundering through the bush until the last one was found. If I was not found first – and I rarely let myself be – I loved the breathless anticipation, my skin crawling with excitement as I waited to be pounced upon.

The noises moved away from me. This bought me extra

time. I wiggled in further – whatever animal used this track, they had fashioned it deep into the otherwise impenetrable scrub. I thought about a wombat, or a fox, scurrying along the path to meet me.

There was a call, louder now, a few yards to my left.

'Found you!' Harriet cried. More heavy sounds through the scrub.

'I saw you, Albert!' she said again, louder now.

Footsteps crashed towards me. I covered my head with my hands and waited to be stumbled over. But the footsteps hurried past and I was safe.

'You're got!' I recognised the voice of my brother James. He was quick to anger and quicker still when it was directed at Albert, I'd noticed, who had arrived and usurped his position as eldest boy. A position made vacant by George that James had never seemed truly able to fill.

Albert laughed. 'Righto – you got me,' he said. So, all he had needed was a game to bring him out of his shell a little.

'Ages ago,' said Harriet, and I sensed the annoyance in her voice. 'Kate,' she called. 'You're the last one. You've won.'

There was no excitement in her voice – just a sharpness, as though Albert had spoiled her last find and now she was bored. This was Harriet's way sometimes. She was the precious only child, and things in her cottage tended to follow Harriet's rhythm. When she was done with the doll, or the game, or the beach we were at, she would become tired. Her loss of interest would rob whatever we were doing of its joy. I wondered what would happen if I stayed hidden. I wondered how long she would search for me.

'Kate! Kate!' the others called. Tumbling shouts that sounded like the cawing of sea birds, echoing out over the cliffs.

I was reminded of the day my own frightened calls had echoed out as I searched fruitlessly for James, who had wandered off when he was on my watch. It had not been long after George died and, as the minutes stretched, my heart grew cold with the thought of what I would say to Mother.

Finally, I had come across the ridgeline and spotted James. He was crouched beside a little black boy, and the two of them were drawing with sticks in the dirt. An older woman – the mother, I assumed – stood close by. I had yelled his name and flown down the ridge, slipping and sliding in the rubble to where he was. They had turned to me, not surprised in the least by my frantic calling. The black woman had raised her head in acknowledgement; we were neighbours of sorts, I suppose – they kept to their place, and we kept to ours. I'd heard the whispered words of Mother and Father, who sometimes spoke about the goings-on inland or down the coast: *murdered, cleared them out, brought them all in.* 'Not here though,' my father had reassured Mother. 'Not on this stretch, my dear. We are quite safe; they are harmless.'

I'd yanked James up that day and growled at him, shooing the mother and her child away. Harmless they may have been, but I wasn't about to take any chances.

My right leg began to cramp, and I tried to stretch it out without rustling too much. Eventually I heard the children tire, one by one, and wander back up to the cottages. I listened to Harriet's admonishment that I'd spoiled an otherwise perfectly good game and to her footsteps as she made to leave, then stopped and returned.

She told Albert to go back without her. I knew that she knew I was capable of playing tricks on her. But she also knew that the cliff edge was right there, that I was foolhardy, a risk-taker.

'Kate, I am deathly serious now. Come out right away, or I'm going to tell your father you have gone over the edge.' Her voice was pinched and high. 'Kate!'

From where I lay I could see her skirt as she paced back and forth through the bush. I couldn't see her face but I wanted to. I wanted to see the worried furrow of her brow, the pinkness creeping up her neck, the way she might be biting down on her lip, pinching it with her teeth.

I waited until she began to cry, a nervous, breathless

teariness. I eased out backwards, as quietly as I could. I could see her near the edge of the cliff, one hand flitting up to push back her hair and then down again to pull at her skirt. I crept up behind her, picking my way through the stones so that the sound did not give me away.

I closed in on her and placed my hands on her waist. 'Found you!' I said in her ear and tickled her hard.

She gasped and whipped around. 'You!' she cried. Without warning she slapped me across the face. 'I thought you had slipped and fallen over. I thought you were dead!'

I held my hand to my stinging cheek. 'It was just a game, Harriet. We were only playing.'

But she pushed me aside and stormed away, towards the cottages.

I walked back slowly and, although the sting of her slap still burned on my face, the chime of her fearful voice as she called my name, the frightened hurt of her words – *I thought you were dead* – warmed me from within.

FIVE

A year passed, punctuated by horseback adventures, and foraging for mussels and crabs at Blackman's Bay or Murray's Beach or one of the many sandy stretches of our cape. The Jacksons settled in, and it was as though they had always been around. Albert and Harry joined us at our desks at the schoolhouse; Mrs Jackson gave birth to another little one, Edward, whom we carried about as our doll when she would let him from her sight. I remember Harriet's hair in plaits. I remember clouds of flour in the kitchen when our mothers left Harriet and me to make scones one afternoon. I remember the first time I realised Harriet had grown taller and slimmer and rounder all at once – and I recall feeling bereft.

It is funny what we choose to remember. And what is forgotten. How some events bed themselves down with permanence; even as they happen, we know that they will be imprinted on our memory forever. And then a scent, a change of season, a recollection of the way the wind was blowing on the day the thing happened will bring it back with such force, that we relive it all over again.

Such is my memory of the night the *SS Alexandria* was wrecked against the rocks the winter I turned eleven.

A storm had been brewing for days, and I'd watched the lines on Father's forehead grow deeper as he wrote in the readings from the barometer while a bank of slate-grey clouds roiled on the horizon. I lay tucked under the bedclothes that night, listening to the wind keen against the sandstone. I could hear things shuddering and clanging in the yard outside. Above all this, I heard the trilling of the telephone line from the light tower and then the shouts of my father.

'Ship down! Man the lifeboats!'

I jumped out of bed and went to the window but could see only the splattering of rain against the pane. Emmaline stirred in her bed.

'What is it?' she said sleepily, and though I know I should have reassured and calmed her, as Harriet might have done were she the big sister, I did not.

'Shipwreck!' I said, and Emmaline leaped up, her eyes wide. It was lucky that Mother rushed in then, otherwise I might have worked Emmaline into a right panic.

'Quickly, girls,' Mother said. 'Emmaline, into my room and to bed at once.' Emmaline scurried over to Mother, who allowed her to nestle into her nightgown for a moment. 'We'll need your room for those they pluck from the water, God willing. Kate, you must go and sleep in with Harriet, come now, put on your coat.'

I hurried into my coat and followed Mother out into the wild night. We had to bend against the wind, and Mother gripped my hand as she held the lantern above her head. She was fearless as the storm whipped around her. A true lighthouse keeper's wife. We huddled in under the porch of the Walkers' cottage, and she rapped at the door.

'Now see you go right to sleep and don't keep Harriet awake with your yabbering,' Mother said as we listened for footsteps in the hall.

Harriet murmured as I slipped in beside her. It was warm under the bedclothes, and they smelled of sleep. I waited until Mrs Walker had pulled the door closed and then I snuggled in against Harriet's back and whispered in her ear. 'A shipwreck, Harriet!'

Her body stiffened, and she rolled over so that her breath, faintly sour, was soft on my cheek.

'Truly?' she asked. 'Is it lost?'

'I don't know.' I pulled my hand free of the blankets and felt in the darkness for her face. Under my fingertips, her lips moved as she spoke.

'Are there many on board? Oh, the poor men.'

'Shush,' I said, and kissed her cheek. I may have been a poor older sister to Emmaline, but I knew how to comfort my Harriet. 'Our fathers will bring them in. Mother will look after them.'

Harriet's body relaxed, and I curled my arm around her shoulders. We stayed like that, our breath mingling and making the air warm between us. Her breathing deepened again, and I felt that this was my duty. To stay awake while the storm raged about us, to keep watch over my friend, just as my father kept watch over all who travelled past our cape. I thought about my mother out there in the darkness and wondered how she had learned to be so brave, to do her job so well. I wondered whether I could ever do as she had done.

She never intended to be the wife of a lighthouse keeper, or so she always told me. But, swept up in the whirl of romance, she did not take heed of her fiancé's hankering for the sea. She was shocked when he knocked on her door a few months into their engagement, brandishing a letter triumphantly.

'I am to be a head lighthouse keeper. We shall be the first family of the light!'

My mother had to sit and fan herself as she processed this news.

'You will love it, Bea, you will make the perfect light keeper's wife,' my father had said.

And when my mother told me this story I could sense the bitter aftertaste in her pride. She *was* the perfect lighthouse keeper's wife. Just as Father presided over the tower and the light and the coastline, Mother took charge of the cottages, the supplies, the animals, we children. She did as she must, for she loved my father and respected his wishes. It's simply – and this thought sometimes snagged at the back of my mind

– that she never wanted to be the wife of a lighthouse keeper on an isolated headland. But who was she to decide her own future?

Mother was dignified in her role. Remained dignified even when she had every reason to grow hard and resentful, even mad with grief. For it was in the rocky earth of this cape that she buried her firstborn, George, before his ninth birthday.

George was, as older brothers are, bossy and sometimes cruel, but I loved him and loved – more than anything – the way he could bring a smile to my mother's face. When George got ill a frown set across mother's brow and it never fully lifted.

I was six when I first knew that George's cough was serious.

'We have to send for a doctor, Tom,' I recall my mother saying. 'It's not just a cough.'

'It might be a week at least before I can get Walters out from town,' my father said. 'By then George'll have broken the fever, no doubt, and we'll all feel foolish and have a pretty penny to pay the doctor for his troubles, too.' My father was kind, but he was practical. I don't think Mother ever forgave him, though – not entirely.

I used to sit with George on the verandah of our cottage.

'Do you ever wonder where all your memories go when you die?' George asked me one day.

'No.' I was clever then, at six, but not that clever.

Unperturbed, he went on. 'I understand what happens to the body, the science of it, decomposing and all that, earth to earth.' He stopped to take a ragged breath. 'And I understand, at least I think I do, what happens to the soul.' At this point my brother had to stop, racked as he was by guttural coughing.

I didn't really understand then what he was saying, but some part of my brain was committing it to memory, so that I could turn it over and over again in the years to come. I stayed quiet until he started again.

'What I don't understand is whether the things that were

in your mind cease to exist when you do. Say, the memory of a pattern I made with the pebbles down on the tideline at Murray's last month.'

'You're not going to die.' It was all I could offer, and I knew he was disappointed.

'We're all going to die.'

'Not if I can help it,' I said, and stalked back inside, not wanting to be around George when he was being so gloomy.

But I thought about our conversation later. I thought about it as I listened to my mother's keening cries, and when the doctor finally came to pronounce the cause of death as pleurisy, not that it was of any use to us. I thought of it when I crept into the hushed room and couldn't bear to lift the starched sheet in the candlelight because, if I didn't lift it, it couldn't be him. And I thought about it when we buried him, and Harriet stood beside me and held my hand, and I whispered to her, 'Where do your memories go when you die?' and she couldn't answer.

I thought about what George had said again that night of the shipwreck as I lay curled around Harriet, and again in the morning when my father's long face at the Walkers' door revealed that men had been lost.

My mother took to her bed that day, exhausted from tending to the injured, but I knew that her grief for her boy had been revived again. I thought about those poor souls drifting out there, their memories unravelling into the deep, dark currents, lost forever. I wished that George had found an answer, or that he would send me a sign telling me where to look for the memories of those who had departed. It would not be the last time I wished such a thing.

SIX

Our education was undertaken in the whitewashed Junction School. The schoolhouse was nestled in a hollow at the junction, halfway between the light station and Bennett's River, where the track wound back over the mountain range towards Edenstown, two days hence. Our teacher, Mr Jamieson, and the shire council chiselled a place of order and discipline out of the wilds around it. We may have run like forest sprites once that last bell of the day sounded, but until then we were perfect examples of the civilising influence of education.

Most of the desks at the Junction School were taken up by us children from the lighthouse, but there were a few children from Bennett's River, too, who were absent as often as they were there. One of these was Davey White, a fisherman's son; people said his mother was on the drink before he was born, which accounted for his being a bit slow.

Mr Jamieson was young and fervent and approached our education as though it were the most important thing in the world. But, some afternoons, as the sun slanted through the windows and one could feel the quiet hum of the waves through the hardwood boards, it was almost impossible to pay attention to him as he read us poems or scratched out the wonder of an equation or tacked a great map to the wall and identified countries for us. Whenever Mr Jamieson pointed out England and then pointed to us – in the colony

– Davey White would gasp and say, 'But why are we at the bottom, sir?'

Of course, my day had always long since begun by the time I made it to my desk. It was my job to check the vegetable patch on the way to the schoolhouse. Harriet always dithered as she got ready and so it was Albert who had taken to joining me on my rounds. We would walk in the dewy bush, soft-soled in the quiet.

There was no soil to speak of on the cape, only sand and rock and grit but, despite this, Mother had insisted on starting a vegetable garden. She and Harriet's mother had worked and worked a piece of ground a half a mile or so inland from the lighthouse. It was tucked in behind a rise, and we watered it with buckets fetched from the little soak close by, which was thick with reeds and the gurgle of frogs.

Over the years Mother and Mrs Walker had collected the goat and horse manure, the kitchen scraps, even, now and then, a pile of kelp they would have one of the horses drag up – Blaze, usually, as she was the most agreeable of the three of them. Sadie was our favourite but older and slower, and Shadow was prone to misbehaviour.

Slowly the sand got some substance and grew darker and started to clump together, and the little vegetable patch was born. What we grew in there mostly came out small and tough, but it was enough, when combined with some of the local plants, the spinach and native currants, to keep our teeth in our heads and the scurvy at bay.

I had to check the fencing around the garden early every morning and make sure there had been no break-in by a kangaroo or a wombat ramming at the wire, trying to get through to the vivid green of the vegetables.

Although I was fairly tall for thirteen, Albert, younger than me by over a year, stood a handspan taller than I did. He was broad in the back and could throw the great logs for the fire around as though they were twigs, but he was still a quiet boy. I always wondered whether the death of his mother when he was so small, and his father's taking up with the new Mrs Jackson, had dented his confidence in some vital way; made him uncertain of his place in the world.

I liked his company nonetheless. If an animal had broken through the fence in the night, I'd have a pile of cleaning up to do, banging the poles back into the soil, mending holes in the wire with smaller pieces threaded in or, if the spot was low to the ground, pieces of timber I forced into the soil to stop the wombats burrowing under. Albert would help and could dig a good hole in half the time I did.

But he didn't treat me like a girl. We just worked at the job until it was done and, if there had been no night invasion, we surveyed the garden, checking to see if purple caterpillars had munched through any of the leaves, or if there was a handful of produce we could take back to the kitchens.

One morning as we came through the ti-tree to the clearing, I noticed movement in the vegetable garden. Ahead, a black girl was stepping over the wire fence. She moved fast; she'd obviously been disturbed at her task. As she went to run, I saw her arms were full of carrots.

'Stop!' I called, before I had time to think.

But she did not stop, just looked my way, momentarily, then ran into the cover of the bush, where I heard her call out to me, guttural and foreign, ending in a laugh.

'Thieving black,' I said angrily, turning to Albert for his agreement, but he had walked on ahead to check the state of the garden. I thought perhaps he hadn't heard me and hurried after him. Albert was a boy of few words, but surely I could count on some level of conversation after an incident such as this.

'Well, what do you think of that then?' I said, coming up next to him, and sounding like my mother.

'Of what?'

'Did you not see the black girl making off with our

37

carrots? The whole crop, I'd reckon. After we've worked so hard.' Albert's dismissal of my annoyance caused it to gurgle and froth within me. 'You don't see them toiling over the earth like we do, trying to make something of it, trying to grow a crop. Not them, wandering around with their babies in the dust and all on show. It's shameless. Thieving! Father won't stand for it.'

'I don't know, Kate.' Albert was careful and quiet and slow. 'You might find he's content to let it go. What's a few carrots, really?'

I looked at him as though he had lost his mind, and turned my attention to the section that had been so messily raided. I kneeled down and started picking at the small stray carrots that had been left behind, raking the soil over with my fingers.

'It's not only the carrots though, is it, Albert?' I stood up. I knew what I wanted to say now and all my righteousness and earnestness came spewing forth. 'It's also the goat last Christmas, and Dot's chickens before that, and the way the wild blacks walk over the cliff near the lighthouse, with nothing but their shirts to hide themselves, laughing at us when we try to hide our eyes and shoo them away.' My face was heating up. 'They should be rounded up like the rest of them and sent down to Lake Myner, where they can learn to be good and decent Christians. Who knows when we might wake up to find that it's more than carrots they've taken? What's to stop them doing what they've done to some of those families further inland? You've heard the stories, Albert – you know as well as I what those men are capable of, what a well-thrown spear can do.'

Let him argue with that.

'They're just stories, Kate. No one's getting speared round here 'less they deserve it, that's what I reckon.' He smiled wryly.

And that was all it seemed I was going to get out of Albert.

'Looks alright,' he added, and started back for the track.

I was fuming and too proud to follow behind so I stomped around the garden for a few minutes more, sensing that I had been laughed at twice this morning, and not liking the feeling at all.

SEVEN

I must have been fourteen when Mrs Jackson, who was pregnant once again, lost a baby. Late one evening Albert came banging on our door.

'It's the baby – it's coming!' I heard him panting to Mother as she pulled on her housecoat.

'Kate,' she called back to me, 'gather some towels and bring them to the Jacksons. Get Mrs Walker on the way.' She hurried out after Albert.

I remembered the births of my brothers and sister, but only in the half-light of a child's memory. I remembered sleeping in Harriet's bed, and Mrs Walker making us porridge in the morning, and going back to our cottage to find Mother in bed with a bundle of blankets at her breast. But until this night, I had never been privy to what happened between the swollen bumps under my mother's dresses and the squashy pink babies that came after.

Mrs Walker and Harriet were already at the door of the Jacksons' cottage when I rushed up. We could hear a muffled wailing coming from inside and let ourselves in. Mr Jackson had made himself scarce, but I could hear Albert reading to Harry and Lucy and little Edward in the front room as we hurried past.

'Doesn't it sound awful?' Harriet whispered.

'Ungodly,' I said.

Mother let us venture as far as the half-closed door of

Mrs Jackson's room before she sent us back to the kitchen to get some water on the boil. I caught a glimpse of strewn bedclothes and the shocking sight of Mrs Jackson's hair come all undone and falling about her shoulders and across her face. Then Mother pulled shut the door.

Harriet and I made the trip between the bedroom and the kitchen so many times that night I lost count. I went outside and filled the pail from the tank and put the kettle on the stove and tidied away the plates and the cups. No doubt Mrs Jackson would find them in the wrong place when she returned to her kitchen and would click her tongue at the fact that I was so inept in matters of the hearth. *That's what you get when you let a girl run wild*, I could almost hear her say.

I tidied and fussed until the screaming reached fever pitch, and then could do nothing but draw a wooden chair next to Harriet's at the table and clutch her hands. The screaming became a rhythmic grunt that sounded like a wild pig, nothing human about it. Harriet and I stared at each other, our eyes wide. I'm certain that Mother and Mrs Walker had forgotten they had left us there in the kitchen, for otherwise they would surely have shooed us away.

Mother's voice carried down the hall, anxiety clear in its cadence. 'Come now, Mary – you're nearly there. One last push.'

This babe would be born very soon, I was sure of it. If I went up the hall, ever so quietly, I might be able to see the moment. Get it clear in my head how this strange women's work got the baby out.

'I'm going up to look,' I said.

'You mustn't,' said Harriet.

'They won't even know I'm there. I'll only peep through the door.'

'Truly, Kate. Think of Mrs Jackson. She'd be mortified.'

'She'll never know I'm there.'

I stood up and moved towards the kitchen door. The grunting rose and fell, and I heard my mother's voice again.

'One more. Hard now. I've got the head but the little one is tiring.'

Behind me, Harriet insisted. 'Don't you do it, Kate.'

But I was on my way. I crept up the hallway to where a faint light fell through the open wedge of doorway. Shadows moved across the walls in there, giant and grotesque.

'Bea,' Mrs Walker murmured to my mother, 'I don't like this colour.'

I wondered what colour she meant as I inched ever closer. I tucked in the shadow next to the doorframe and stared into the bedroom.

Mother and Mrs Walker had their backs to me as they crouched at the foot of the bed. And Mrs Jackson: well, Harriet needn't have worried she would see me, for all I could see of her were her knees high and naked on the bed and beyond that her white face pressed sideways into the pillow, looking away from me.

As my mother and Harriet's shifted in the low light, I saw what it was they concentrated on. The gaping space between Mrs Jackson's thighs. A space that, even from my hiding spot, I could tell was grotesquely rearranged with a bloody white circle at its centre.

I squeezed my eyes shut, but an unearthly moan caused me to open them again. I watched as that bloody white circle grew larger, and I wondered how Mrs Jackson could be still living and have this thing coming out of her ... from there!

Then in a great rush a small body sluiced out in a bloody mess, and Mother grabbed it and held it over her arm and appeared to push and push against its back.

Mrs Jackson asked, 'What is it? Why doesn't it cry? Where's the baby?'

Mrs Walker hurried to hold Mrs Jackson's hand and smooth back her brow, and my mother kept pushing against the baby, all mottled white and blue, as she held it over her arm.

'Come now, come now,' Mother mumbled and pushed again and again.

After a time, Mrs Walker came to my mother's side. She laid her hand on her arm and said, low and gentle-like, 'No more, Bea.'

My breath seized in my throat.

Mother pushed once more and then bowed her head. She whispered a prayer. 'Hail Mary, full of grace …'

I slipped back to the kitchen and to Harriet's wide and questioning eyes.

It was impossible to get to sleep that night. Everything I'd seen swirled in my mind, and I was sick and sad and guilty all at once.

I could not ask Mother as she ushered me home to our cottage and to bed, for her face was closed and blank, and she did not, of course, realise I had witnessed the shocking scene. But I heard her as I tossed and turned and tried to get to sleep. She was weeping. Thinking, I suppose, of Mrs Jackson's babe who'd been lost before he even took a breath. And thinking, too, of her own boy, her baby once.

The next week, as we trod quietly around the Jacksons and their awkward sadness, the pounding in my head and deep throb in my centre revealed itself as the brown heavy blood of my first curse. I was shocked, but then pleased.

In truth I had been wishing for this, ever since Harriet had told of hers twelve months back. I had sulked for a time that she would get it before I did, even though I knew full well that she had no control over such a thing at all. It seemed to accentuate the gap in our ages, which had hardly ever mattered at all. I wondered if this blood would mark the same change in me that I had witnessed in Harriet: a blossoming, luminous quality, a gentle swell under her skin that made her seem infinitely older than me.

My mother surprised me in the laundry as I was trying to rinse out my undergarments. She must have known at once why I was there.

'Has it come, then?' she said.

I nodded but did not look up, relieved that she would now take me with a sure hand and tell me what to do.

'That's good and healthy. When you're finished up here, come into my room and we'll get you sorted out.'

'Thank you,' I said, meeting her eyes.

'You know what it means, don't you, Kate?'

I did and I didn't. I knew it was a line I was crossing, from childhood to adulthood, and I wanted to stay and I wanted to go, and I wanted to be able to be in both places forever more.

'You're getting ready to make babies.'

My jaw dropped.

'Not right away, of course! It's the body's way of saying that everything is working and that you'll be a mother one day, is all.'

Harriet had not said. Of all the secret, whispered things I thought might be revealed by this event, this was not one of them. The knowledge of it stole something from me. Stole the careless way in which I had considered my body until now. And my blood became linked in my mind with the blood of Mrs Jackson, talk of babies with dead babies; and every time I felt that cursed cramp and heaviness, anxiety pressed in on me.

I realised then what a burden I carried as a girl, as a woman, and could not believe Harriet had not prepared me better.

EIGHT

It was a few weeks later that I first heard the name McPhail. I was at home, no longer eligible for school because I would turn fifteen that year. My days were now filled up with fetching and mending and washing and baking and hanging out the laundry. Harriet was thrilled that I had finally left the schoolhouse and joined her.

Sometimes we would plead with our mothers to relieve us of our chores and, if they agreed, we would whoop and yahoo as we raced down the hill away from the station to hide ourselves on one of our favourite beaches. Every so often, I would long for my brain to be tried and tested as it had been by Mr Jamieson's lessons, and I would sneak away from both Mother and Harriet, to be with one of my books.

But this particular day was not one for books. Mother and I were serving tea and scones to Dot Appleton, who had brought eggs and fresh gossip. She had it from Mr Jamieson who heard from Mr Prucherp from Bennett's River that a man, not young but not old, was moving to the area.

Daniel McPhail was his name. He'd come from somewhere out bush in New South Wales and was looking to take up the abandoned hut down at the cove. Apparently he'd been left it in a will, but no one could remember who'd last lived there or why on earth someone would journey out all this way to claim it. No wife. No children. Just him and a swag and a want for someone to buy the fish he planned to catch.

Mother made interested noises and asked me to fill the kettle again. By the time I returned and placed the full kettle back on the stove, the women had moved on to another tale.

'Met him just today on the road back from the junction. Nice enough,' my father said that evening. 'Tall – good hands – he'll do well enough for himself with the fishing if he's as good as he makes out. Been a long while, but he said the sea had never left him, that he was itching to get back out.'

I had finished washing my face and was heading for bed, but I stopped in the hall. I could hear Mother at the dishes.

'He's already talked to the men from Bennett's River,' Father continued. 'They reckon there's a small boat going from when Tommy McGregor got sick and gave it up. This McPhail thinks he's got the coin to buy it straight out. Reckons he can keep us in fish. The men from down there will work the coast the other way and not have to bother about getting round here to us.'

'And what about Blackwell? He's been keeping us in fish alright till now.'

Father snorted. 'Blackwell spends as much time catching flies with his drunken mouth as he does catching fish! I told McPhail if he got up here with his catch first then we'd welcome it and keep him in tea and sugar and flour.'

'Your decision, dear,' Mother said.

I knew I should go to bed, but there was something in the name, even then, that caught me like a tiny silver hook.

'I told him there weren't much but the fish and the sea and the bush and the wind. He'd come to the wrong place if he was looking for drinking companions, or to find a woman to keep his hearth and his bed warm.'

'Tom!'

'Men's words, my love; it's how it goes.' My father's voice was bright. 'He said that suited him fine – that he'd had enough of women. That sea and fish and a fire in his hut would keep him warm enough.'

'He'll have a past he's running from sure enough, then,' Mother said, clattering the dishes into their rack above the bench.

'That may be so, my love, that may be so.' Mother laughed quietly, and my father's footsteps sounded on the boards, as he added, 'And it's no business of ours what business a man might be running from.'

Mother's answer was muffled.

I crept back up the hall to my bedroom where I could mull over the fact of this new arrival to the cape.

I didn't have long to wait before I saw him in the flesh.

I was in the washhouse beating the soap out of the sheets and entreating Emmaline to hold fast to her end of the tangle, lest the whole lot fall onto the floor and we'd have to start again.

'You pull too hard!'

'You're weak,' I muttered.

'What did you say?' She tugged hard at the sheets so that I lost my balance.

'Don't be such a child!' I said, and wrenched the sheets back.

'I. Am. Not. A. Child!' She tugged the sheet hard with each word.

'Are too!' I loosened my grip so that she relaxed a little. Then I pulled sharply, and she lost her footing and fell onto the dirt floor of the washhouse.

She yelled as she scrambled up, and I dumped the sheets back in the tub and raced out the door, shrieking as I went. I knew she would give me a right pummelling if she got to me. I probably deserved it.

I raced around the corner of the washhouse, laughing, and heard her slam the laundry door and follow on my heels. I ran towards the fence line and slipped behind the goat shed, thinking I might lose her that way. But her footsteps kept coming, along the other side of the shed.

'You can't hide from me!' she called, and I shrieked and ducked out from behind the shed.

'You'll never catch me!' I paid no heed at all to my flying skirts, my arms helter skelter, my hair unpinned, as I ran straight into a man.

Heaven only knows what he thought when I came around that corner and fairly landed in his arms.

I pulled up fast, shocked, and a big hand clamped on my shoulder to steady me.

'Whoa there,' he said, and I looked up at him. He had a broad face framed with thick dark hair. Grey eyes, like the sea at dusk. He wore a beard, quite short but full and thick. He did not smile but was not severe. Perhaps I amused him, for his eyes widened a little as I stepped back from his grasp.

'Thank you,' I said. 'I am fine.' My breath was all ragged, and I could not get my mind to still, jumping around as it was, at this man before me, the sensation on my shoulder where his hand had been.

'I see that,' he said.

I heard Emmaline come to an abrupt halt behind me. I turned my head, reluctantly I'll admit, for it was not often that dark strangers arrived on our cape, and scowled at Emmaline. She, in all her childishness, clapped both hands over her mouth and erupted in a fit of giggles before she slunk away behind the goat shed.

'McPhail,' he said, and I whipped my head back to face him. 'I'm after the head keeper.'

So this was the man. Of course it was. I found myself looking at his hands. I sensed a blush begin to creep up my neck.

'That's my father.'

I made no move, and we stood there together. Only a couple of hand spans between us. For everything that came after, I have held the fact of it warm in my heart: *I saw him first, Harriet, I saw him first.*

48

'Your father?' He tilted his head to one side.

'Yes,' I said. 'Come with me and I'll show you to the work shed. He's in there. They have not sent the part. The part that was to come for the light, that is. He's had to make do, which he does very well, of course, being the head keeper, but he wouldn't normally ...' I was babbling, I knew it, for the words tumbled out, fast and unmatched and not fitting together as they should. I fell quiet.

He followed a few steps behind me as we crossed the yard. I looked over my shoulder once, twice, but he seemed to pay me no heed. We approached the shed, and I called out to Father. He appeared in the doorway, raising his hand to his hat when he saw the man.

'Ah, McPhail. You've had the pleasure of meeting my daughter then?

'Indeed.'

'What brings you to the station today?'

'I'm in need of a saw, if you have one to spare for a few days.'

'That I do,' said my father. 'It'll cost you though.'

McPhail raised his chin and kept his eyes steady on my father.

'I'll take a salmon next week, if they're biting,' Father said, and smiled.

McPhail loosened his stance and nodded, a glint in his eye.

I was taken aback by the fact that this man did not seem to place any particular regard on my father's position as head keeper. Often when men from Bennett's River came by they appeared to bow their heads before Father. It made him uneasy but it seemed to me to keep order in the world.

I hung outside the shed while McPhail and Father did their business, talking the foreign tongue of tools and lengths and what was required to fix the little hut. When they emerged, they shook hands, and Father turned to me.

'Still here? Are you waiting to show our visitor out?' He chuckled, and I blushed.

'Of course not.' I knew the red in my cheeks grew ever brighter.

McPhail glanced at me. 'No need – I'll be off.' He began to walk away. 'My thanks again.' He tipped his hat and strode towards the track that led down to the cove.

He had not even asked my name.

NINE

It was decided that Harriet and I were to have new dresses. At least, our old dresses needed letting out. Mine especially, for it was as though my flesh had suddenly unloosed itself from my frame and was bulging and curving in ways it had not before.

It was after dinner, and Mother and Mrs Walker sat up under the lamplight in our parlour, chapped hands running over their tiny stitches as they tried to fashion something new out of something old; nipping in a waist here, puffing a sleeve there.

I stood on the piano stool while Mother lowered the hem on my dress; I had grown four inches since last spring. I liked the feel of a dress being pinned and buttoned up around me but I struggled to keep as motionless as Harriet did.

Mother, lips held stiff over the ends of a silvery row of pins, muttered, 'Kate, I'll put a pin in you if you don't hold still.'

I craned my neck to catch a glimpse of my reflection in the window. All those pleats and buttons and puffs made a new shape out of me in a way that I couldn't quite comprehend. I usually tried to avoid the mirror, which would reflect all the bursting new flesh back at me. Harriet, of course, had become a more elegant version of herself, while I felt somehow unrecognisable.

Harriet stood on one of the kitchen chairs she'd dragged in. Hers was a smooth silhouette, tucked in at the waist and curving into the proper shape at the chest, whereas Mother always told me that I looked as if I'd been wrestled into each dress she made me.

Mother poked at me and demanded again that I stand still, for the pins were all coming unstuck where I stretched.

'For the love of God, Kate Gilbert,' Mother said, 'how will we ever make a lady of you?'

She shook her head, and Mrs Walker laughed softly with her.

'Whoever said I wanted to be?'

'Here we go again!'

The two mothers smiled knowingly at each other.

'Well, some days, I'm just not sure that I'm cut out for the life of a lady. I mean, who will ever marry a wild girl of the cape anyway?'

Mrs Walker spoke up. 'Now, Kate, that's not true at all, I know plenty of young men who will think you marriage material, when you come of age. Mr Walker and I are thinking of sending Harriet to Melbourne, possibly at the end of the year, once she's seventeen, to stay with her aunt. See what she can turn up in the city.'

I saw the shadow of a frown pass across Mother's forehead. It was only momentary, but I wondered whether it was fear or envy that creased it so.

'You'll both be married off soon enough and we'll be left with two fewer sets of hands to take the load and two fewer pairs of ears to listen to our tales,' Mother said.

It was obvious from her face that Harriet had not heard a word since her mother had mentioned the suitors who might be found in Melbourne. Was Harriet imagining a long line of gentlemen, fresh with youth and taut with anticipation, in their dark morning suits and fine top hats, a line stretching out down the busy streets of Melbourne? Maybe she saw herself, a fair maiden escaped from the bleak cape who now spent her days peeking coyly from a window as her aunt received the compliments of each man. Maybe one man, confident and handsome, would glance up and catch her eye, and it would be love, true and divine, and all would be well, forever after. What poppycock!

'Perhaps I will never leave you, Mother,' I said. 'Perhaps no suitors will ever come for me, or perhaps I'll not receive any if they do. Perhaps Father will teach me the trade and I'll become the first female lighthouse keeper of this Great Southern Land.'

At this, all three of them broke into laughter.

I bristled. 'Perhaps, I won't stay after all. Why could I not go to Melbourne, if Harriet does, and see the grand theatres, the library, the bustling city? What stops me from boarding a ship and setting sail for Europe and touring the great cities of the world and reading their literature and hearing their foreign tongues, and seeing the remnants of the birth of civilisation?'

My speech was all garbled now, words spilling out on top of each other. I thought myself so very mature, a few months shy of fifteen, and so full of ideas about my place in the world, my singular potential, my possible greatness, that I had no room for the knowing smiles of the mothers, the blank look of Harriet, who had endured my rants before.

'Perhaps,' said my mother.

In perfect synchronicity, as if they had some secret code, both mothers set down their pins and scissors.

'Enough for tonight. We can finish these tomorrow,' Mother said.

Harriet and I slid carefully out of the pinned dresses and drew shawls over our underthings.

'To bed then, girls,' Mrs Walker said.

Harriet and I brushed our cheeks against each other's, and I squeezed her hand.

I retired to my room and turned up the lamp, ignoring Emmaline's huffing from the other bed. The conversation had disquieted me, and I needed to lose myself in a book to settle my thoughts. I was reading *The Water Babies* again. How I loved the delicious greens and blues of its cover, split by a banner with a kelp-brown title. Fat silvery fish slid across the book jacket and peered around the spine, and a trio of water nymphs floated amid the centre of the image in dresses that seemed spun from water. In the foreground, a black-haired boy kneeled on all fours, head turned towards the ghostly sea-girls as they shimmered in the distance. Even Harriet had been impressed the day it arrived from her aunt, and had flicked through it as though she might be interested in such a beautiful thing. She soon found she wasn't, and returned to leafing through her magazines.

For a time I was obsessed with the idea that I could live under the sea. Not in one of those strange and ugly-looking diving dresses I had seen pictures of in the paper, nor using a great tank of air strapped to my neck. No, I wanted to dive deep down, skimming the sandy bottom of the ocean with my bare skin. I wanted to glide through fingers of pink weed and velvety fronds of green and come face to face with a mullet, or a gummy shark, slide up to the rubbery flank of a great whale and feel her song vibrate through my cheek to the very centre of my brain and understand what she told me.

These were the peculiar thoughts I never shared with Harriet, or anyone else. There seemed to be an aspect of my interior world that troubled others. When I let slip a flight of fancy or a curious question, others would stare at me as though I were absurd. Sometimes I felt as if there were something amiss in my make-up. That all the pieces had not been put together right.

You couldn't see it from the outside – no, it was my inside that was awry. It made me recoil at the thought of marriage, made me dream of sailing away, of living beneath the ocean. Sometimes on the rocks you could get within a foot of a dead seal, if the wind was blowing away from you. The rocks would obscure it, and you could be right over it, about to step into the putrefying flesh, before you inhaled the unholy whiff of it and realised you'd been breathing it in all along. That's all that was needed for me to be found out; a wind change, and someone would sense what was rotten inside of me.

I focused on the words again and tried not to think of such things.

TEN

The very first time we went to McPhail's hut was because of the rain. Or at least that's what I told myself. Big, fat rain that dropped between the leaves in sheets.

We'd known it might come; that morning we'd seen the clouds curdling in the south. There had been a flapping urgency to the washing going out, in steaming heaps, wrung and stretched across the lines. But it had been days since Harriet and I had escaped. We pretended we didn't hear our mothers calling for us to come and help.

It was a trek to get down to the white curve of beach at the cove. Back out along the rutted track that stuck to the ridge, and then sharply down to follow a watercourse that seeped through the thick banksia and the blue-green eucalypts.

It usually took us the best part of two hours to make the journey on foot and, by the time we reached the sand that day, whatever sun there had been was hidden deep in grey cloud. We were not inclined to even paddle.

Instead, we tucked ourselves in behind a little dune to eat our thick slices of bread smeared with plum jam and then lay in the nodding grasses with our heads together, watching the sky through the feathery tips. Sometimes there was no need for talking. Sometimes sea and sky and grass and Harriet and a bellyful of bread and jam was all I could ever imagine I would want.

And then came the rain. Whipping in, cold and heavy and

all at once, so that we ran, squealing, for the cover of the trees back behind the beach. Even there, though, we could find no protection from the drenching wet of it. It grew dark and thunder vibrated over the sea, booming in waves as it came in over the land.

'We have to find somewhere to shelter!' cried Harriet as lightning cut the sky above us.

'Come on!' I yelled, grabbing her hand and heading further into the bush. 'This way!'

I knew that his hut was close. I could say that we stumbled across it but, ever since I had bowled into the man that day near the sheds, I had wanted to meet him again. I told myself later that the walk and the rain were fate's way of pushing us towards him. I told myself that, but I don't think it was true.

'There, ahead, Harriet! The fisherman's hut!'

I could see smoke sputtering valiantly out of a chimney and the windows all aglow. I noticed her hesitate beside me at the sight, but we were wet through, and the rain still fell and it seemed we really had no choice at all.

Oh, what he must have thought when we arrived, dripping like drowned rats as we knocked on his door.

'Can we come in?' I had to say, once McPhail opened the door and stood staring at us.

Harriet was trembling a little beside me – I could feel it through her sleeve – and I thought she was cold but, then again, it may not have been that. This was the first time she had seen the man.

McPhail broke his silence. 'Right, of course,' he said. 'Come in.' He tucked his hair, stiff with salt, behind his ears. Even as we stepped into the hut, the briny scent of him was everywhere. Something beat like a little trapped fish high and fast in my chest.

He gestured that we should sit down at a small table and asked if we would have tea.

We hesitated before we sat for there were only two chairs. He stood near the stove, waiting for the billy to boil. We rested at the table, bodies angled in towards the heat. Every few seconds we would steal a glance across at each other and stifle a giggle.

There was steam coming off the skirts of my dress where they were closest to the stove. The thrum of the rain and the crack of the thunder outside made the storm seem very close and the hut very small. I could have crossed it in three big steps.

There was a table in the centre of the room, the little stove on one wall opposite the door. Against the wall to my left was a long bench, with two shelves running behind, planks of wood propped on bricks. On the shelves were some tins, and odds and ends, grimy and stacked upon each other – a wooden spoon, a length of rope, a jar of hooks, a small painted portrait in a frame. Against the other wall were a thin cot and a wooden cupboard, a rifle propped at its side. A heavy oilskin hung from the cupboard door.

McPhail twisted the lid off a tin, shook leaves into the bubbling water, then took the billy from the heat. He let it stand upon the wood block on the table. There were only two tin mugs. Harriet undid the first three buttons of her bodice and patted at the skin there on her neck with her handkerchief.

McPhail looked up from the pot. 'Sugar?'

We nodded.

He poured the tea and scooped in three spoons of sugar each, then moved to the shelves and took down a bottle. Even with his back to us, I saw him take a swig of the tannin liquid. I felt bold.

'Can I have some of that?'

'Kate!' warned Harriet.

'Your father won't thank me for that,' he said, glancing at me.

'My father gives me a glass every now and then, for Christmas and the like.' His eyes on me made me bolder still. 'I'm the head keeper's daughter, you know. I'm Kate.'

'We've met.'

'And this is Harriet.'

Did I make it happen, I wonder? By saying her name out loud, sitting there in the crackling warmth of the stove, under the heaving noise of the storm. Was I like one of the witches in *Macbeth*, stirring the future with my words?

Harriet looked up properly then, and he held out his hand for her to shake.

'Daniel McPhail,' he said, the corner of his mouth hitching up ever so slightly.

Once he'd turned back to the fire, saying we'd be better to wait out the storm and then he'd see us home, I noticed that Harriet's face was lit up, as if the fire were in her and not in the hearth.

ELEVEN

Without ever acknowledging it to each other, Harriet and I started to turn our attention to the cove for our adventures. Before, we had liked to vary our walks, sometimes to the furthest jetty, or the point, or down to Murray's Beach. Now we took the same path over again. It did not provide us with so much as a sighting of McPhail until two weeks after that day in the hut.

We were stretched out, toes wriggling in the sand, when the shot echoed down to the cove. We both turned our heads at the same time, peering back into the shadows of the trees.

'What was that?'

'Sounded like a gun.' I was up, brushing the sand from my skirts. 'Let's go see.' I started towards the tree line before Harriet had a chance to quarrel.

'But we don't know who it is. Or … or what they might be doing.' Harriet hurried after me, picking up our boots and stockings and swinging them in her hands.

'We'll find out then, won't we?'

'But what if they fire again?'

'We'll be careful.' I raised my arm to shield my face from the sun. 'Maybe it's the fisherman – he might be shooting his supper instead of hooking it today?'

Harriet stopped and stared at me, then hurried on. 'Oh, do you think?' she said, as though it were no matter to her at all.

We saw him before he saw us. He was crouched down in

a clearing with his back towards us. The gun lay on the stony ground next to him. He had taken off his shirt and wore only a thin cotton vest. His shoulders were moving rhythmically, as if he were sawing and, as he lifted one hand up to his face, wiping away sweat and flies, I noticed a smear of blood up his forearm.

Next to me, Harriet put her hand on her chest and breathed in sharply. I went forwards to get a better look at what lay in front of him, and the sound of my brushing through the trees made him pause, raise his head and turn it sharply.

'What in heaven's name?' he said, as he stood up and faced me.

'We heard a shot,' I said, taking in the blood spattered down the front of his vest and across his pants, his chest heaving a little with exertion and surprise, the dead kangaroo with its stomach slit to reveal a glistening pile of purple viscera.

'We heard the shot,' I said again, my voice coming out thin and high, my throat constricting with nerves.

He was looking to the side of me now, and I could hear Harriet stepping through the underbrush behind me.

In his right hand he held a knife, tucked in next to his leg as if, perhaps, we might not notice it. Across the silver blade was a thick crimson streak.

'This is no business for ladies.' McPhail nodded his head at Harriet, ever so slightly, as he turned away from us. 'You'd best run along now.' He bent down and went back to his sawing.

'What will you do with it?' I tried to sound daring, but inside I was leaning out too far from the top balcony of the lighthouse and peering into the swirling whitewater below.

McPhail paused. 'I'll eat it.'

Maybe he expected us to run away, but I wasn't leaving now.

'What does it taste like?' I'd always refused the dark meat when Mother had been forced to serve it up if our stocks ran low and Father had brought her a carcass from the bush

61

instead of the storeroom. Now my refusal seemed infantile and squeamish.

I sensed Harriet's gaze on me. I think she was nervous and impressed, both at the same time. It had been one thing, to run to the hut in the storm, to take shelter, to be served tea, but this was something else.

The birds sent up a clattering racket in the canopy above us; I thought I could smell the warm wetness of the kangaroo's innards.

McPhail went back to carving up the carcass, but this time he kept talking. 'A bit tough, but good, meaty. Mrs Everett in Bennett's River – her husband's poorly and she asked that I bring her some meat if I could.'

'Can we watch?'

'Like I said, it's no business for ladies.' I couldn't be sure, but it sounded as if he were smiling. 'Though, you don't seem like one to be put off.' He looked up at me directly.

Grabbing Harriet's hand I moved towards where McPhail was squatted over the carcass.

The animal wasn't a large male like I'd seen standing guard over mobs before. This one was smaller – a female I noted from the loose flap of pouch that had been sliced through. She faced away, eyes rolled back to the white, as if she couldn't bear to watch him take her apart.

I crouched down like McPhail and pulled Harriet with me.

His big hands gripped the knife as he hacked at the leg joint; I noticed a blue-grey vein pulse in his neck. It thrilled me. There was a cracking sound, and a spray of bright blood spurted up. Harriet gasped, and I reared my head back, surprised by the sudden shoot of it, as though the animal were still alive.

I glanced at Harriet and saw a fine spray of red across her cheek.

McPhail was looking, too. He gestured towards his own cheek and said, 'You've … here.' The phrase seemed to escape him. 'On your cheek.'

Harriet's white hands fluttered in front of her face, and she made a strange noise.

I pulled a handkerchief from my bodice and reached out to wipe the smear away; the blood was bright on the lace and, as much as I tried afterwards to remove it, the stain was there for good. I found the handkerchief again, much later, and I folded it away to keep.

It took the best part of the afternoon for McPhail to carve up that kangaroo. When he was finished, a canvas sack bulged at his feet. He was neat and methodical; he'd wrapped the dribbling pile of guts in paper and tucked them in the sack – good for catching sharks, he told us – and all that remained was a bloodied patch of ground.

As we made to leave, knowing we would already be late home for supper, gathering our skirts as the afternoon's light unravelled in the sky above us, Harriet paused, and I watched her place her hand gently on McPhail's forearm, darkened with grime and blood.

'It's kind, your taking the meat to Mrs Everett. She'll be ever so grateful.' And she left her hand there, a second longer than she ought.

I would always wonder, when I had cause to return to the scene again and again in my mind: how did she know that one touch, placed just so, was all that was needed?

TWELVE

Ever since our meetings with McPhail, Harriet had come over all dreamy. We were helping in the washhouse one morning, a week or so after the incident with the kangaroo, when she stuck her hands straight into the copper right after it had come off the heat. She yelped and snatched them out as I pulled her towards the laundry trough.

'Harriet, what were you thinking?' I said as I plunged her pink and steaming hands into cold water.

'I mustn't have been thinking at all,' she replied as she winced, and the water splashed over her skin.

'You're ever so distracted.'

'Am not,' she said swiftly, and I noted her haste.

Harriet was ordered inside to rest and endure a salve applied to her hands, but I stayed in the washhouse, stirring the tubs and wondering what was preoccupying her mind. Perhaps it was a fisherman's hand as it prepared tea in a billy, or sawed the flesh of a kangaroo.

All through the next week she continued to be distracted and refused all my offers to escape to the cove or for a walk, once our chores were done.

After one such rejection, I muttered, 'Let me know when you do have time for me, Harriet; when you've finished mooning over that stupid fisherman.'

'Kate!' she snapped, no doubt more afraid of the fact that I'd spoken the thought out loud where any of the children might hear and tattle about a tiff between the two big girls. Especially if they tattled that it involved a fisherman.

The men around us were basically family, and those who lived on the periphery of the lighthouse, at Bennett's River and beyond, were outsiders: fishermen, loners, hermits. There was an unspoken understanding that it would be none of these men who wooed us and asked for our hand.

Even the brittle way in which my mother greeted Albert and me sometimes when we returned from the vegetable garden was enough for me to realise that there was a threat that had arrived with my coming of age. It was to do with my body, my womanhood, the electricity that I sensed every now and then with a sideways glance from Albert, or when lying in a sandy nook with Harriet, our skirts pulled up past our knees. Were all these things the same? Did they threaten the good order of the cape, of me, of the world in the same way?

The following day, as if in penance, Harriet asked me to join her for a picnic at the point.

'Please, Kate. I even had Mother make us currant buns. I've found lemon cordial and bread and cheese … the sun is out. Will you come?'

'Well, I suppose we haven't been down there in a while …' I wanted to make her plead. It felt good to have her focus on me so completely again. Her attention made me alive.

'Come on, I've made sure all the other children are busy – no one will follow us.'

I took her outstretched hand and ran with her, the satchel carrying our picnic lunch bumping between us.

The point was a knobby finger of rock that jutted out into the sea not far from the lighthouse. The cliffs hung over the rocks so that we had to walk a few bays further along the top and then clamber down and rock-hop back to the point. The rocks were jagged in some places, sticking up sharply so that we had to be careful not to twist our ankles as we stepped between them. The landscape changed then and gave way to huge boulders, orange lichen growing over them like onion skin, wedged in place, creating crevices, nooks, shady caves where we could sit and hide and while away an afternoon.

The adventure of the point was that you could only get all the way around when the tide was low; there was a deep gully that led back to a cave, and beyond it a sheer wall of rock. When the tide was in, the gully was awash with foamy water, surging and gurgling, sucking into the space and then rushing back out, fast and furious. If you got caught in it, you didn't stand a chance.

The width of the gully at the spot we crossed was only about four feet; two sure-footed hops across the backs of round rocks. As you approached the gully, if you knew it as we did, you could just make out a couple of indentations on the rock wall on the other side, enough space to get a toe in and be able to push yourself up and over the top, to the great expanse of the point, a long sloping slab of rock, smooth and always warm with the soaked-up sun.

Where the rock sloped into the water, it created a deep green pool. On a good day, when there was enough cloud so that there was no reflection and no wind to rumple the skin of the water, you could see all the way to the sandy bottom. Arrowed fish in triangles darted across the pool, and swathes of kelp swayed in and out with the current. Clustered along the tide line were the fat, black shapes of sea slugs, glistening as they waited for the water to come back up and cover them.

Crusting the sides of the pool, and scratching the backs of our legs as we dangled our feet in the water, were hundreds upon hundreds of barnacles, some striped, some a faded blue. We could lie on that sloping rock, protected in the lee of a ledge for hours upon hours. Counting the beats between sprays as the waves shlocked into the point, following with our fingers the seagulls wheeling and diving above our heads.

On this day, the tide was low, the gully easy, and as Harriet spread out our picnic lunch, I unlaced my boots, relishing the feel of the rock under the soles of my feet.

'Lemon cordial must be the most delicious drink on this

earth, don't you think?' Harriet said as she lifted the canteen to her lips, and wiped the drips from her mouth with the back of her hand. 'Sweet and sour and wonderful.'

I'd lain down with my chin resting on my arms so that the rock didn't chaff against my skin. 'I dare say there are more delicious drinks, Harriet.'

She was attempting to engage me in one of my favourite games of the imagination. She did not care for them as much as I, but it warmed me that she would throw out a line for me to catch like this.

'Consider if you will, the sparkling apple wine of the northern mountains of France,' I said, playing along.

'The northern mountains of France, you say? And who taught you that, you ignorant girl! What about the molten chocolate drink of the Amazon, served with gold leaf and the native berries of the rainforest?'

I flipped over onto my back, feeling the delight in our banter fill my chest until I wanted to shout: *I've missed you, Harriet! I've missed you!* But I didn't, and instead I carried on our game, and we laughed and licked our lips as we described the strange concoctions of our minds.

We wrapped the remains of our picnic in the cloth and roamed along the shadowed cove where a little shaly beach had formed, made by layer upon layer of bleached shells.

I wandered back and forth on the little beach, searching for special shells, slowly pacing each step so that I would not miss a buried treasure. Those shells that caught my eye I stooped to examine, stretching out my finger to unearth the piece, checking to see if it was whole. If it pleased me, I would place it on a flat grey rock that sat up in the centre of the little beach. I liked to find a pattern to my collecting: a colour, a curve, a texture, a size.

While I was engaged in my task, Harriet sat cross-legged on the beach, smoothing a space in the shale in front of her with the side of her hand. She had made a little pile of round white shells, each about the size of a shilling. These were the doors of mollusc shells, a spiral etched on one side of them. She began to make a pattern with them, chatting away to me as she did so; I think we were discussing the wardrobe of Mr Eagleton, who had recently visited to check on the mechanics of the light, when Harriet gave away the deeper contents of her thoughts.

'Do you suppose it's true what they say about McPhail?' she said, never lifting her eyes from the careful shape she was creating.

'What who says?' I said, after a pause.

'I overheard Mother and Father.' She twirled a white shell in her fingers. 'They said he fell from grace, that he was engaged to marry, that his heart has been broken?'

'Well, it makes a good story, doesn't it?' I traced back along the ground I hadn't covered yet. 'I suspect that, as with any good story, there are elements of truth and the rest has been made up to suit the storyteller.'

'But why would they make up a story like that?' Harriet seemed both perplexed and annoyed that the conversation hadn't been as neat as she anticipated.

I believed what I was saying, that there was a bitter space between the truth and the story that was told. I knew it in the way my parents sometimes answered my questions in a calm and measured manner when I knew full well they had been fighting about the very same thing only moments before. I knew it from how Harriet hedged and sighed her way around the change in herself, the way she'd been snagged on the thought of McPhail and the fact that she couldn't say it out loud.

'I suppose there was some kind of fall from grace for him to be living out here,' I said. 'I suppose there was money and women and brushes with danger and death. I suppose there was all of that because that's what happens in life.' I threw a broken shell to the side. 'At least, that's what I suppose happens. It's hard to tell when one's life has been confined to this cape.'

Harriet said nothing, and I decided to probe a little further into her thoughts.

'Why do you worry about the truth of McPhail's story, Harriet? It is no business of ours, surely, what lies in his past?'

There was a long silence from Harriet, and I counted the splash of the waves as they broke over the lip of rock: *one, two, three, four*.

'He is our neighbour, of sorts. I only think it's right to know the things that might help us better understand the man – that's all.'

'Can I speak plainly, Harriet?'

'You always do.'

I directed my words not at Harriet but out to sea, so that their impact might be tempered by the space between.

'I think that you have become quite enamoured of the fisherman. I think that maybe you harbour feelings for him that you believe are not ones that you should.'

'That's not true.' A brittle edge to her voice.

'Do you love him?'

'Love him?' Harriet's response came out in a rush. 'Love him? How could I love him? He is at least fifteen years my senior. A fisherman! He lives in that tiny little hut and kills kangaroos with his bare hands – he is barely above a savage! Love the man – I think not.' Her face had gone a strange shade of pink, and her words fairly flew from her mouth.

'If you say so,' I said, leaving it, for she had told me all I needed to know, and all I wondered now was why she was refusing to discuss the maelstrom of her true feelings with me.

I stood up then. The sounds of the waves hitting the rock seemed to be coming in a little faster and stronger. The surface of the pool was swirling with whitewater now, and the black sea slugs had all but vanished under the rising water.

'Harriet, we have to go – the tide.' I scrambled to pack the pile of wrapped picnic things in the satchel, pulling my boots back on and shoving my shells deep into my pocket.

Although she was sulkily quiet after my interrogation,

Harriet hastened after me, knowing full well that we would be stuck or face an arduous climb and trek to get back to the station before dark if we failed to cross the gully before the tide covered our path.

I heard the deep sloshing noise of the gully even before I peered over the edge. The surface of our rock was already submerged under two or three inches of water.

'Quick, Harriet,' I called over my shoulder as I twisted around to shimmy down the rock face.

I propped myself on a ledge that remained clear of the water and waited for a break in the waves. Father had taught me that they usually came in sets, enough of a pattern that I knew I could expect a smaller wave every now and then. Harriet was panting behind me, and I knew that she wouldn't be confident crossing the gully and having to splash on to the slippery rocks.

'Harriet, I'm going to go in the next break. The pull is strong and you'll need to move fast.' She nodded, her lips pressed tightly together. 'Move down to this ledge when I'm gone and wait for me to tell you when to go.' I reached up and squeezed her hand. 'You'll be fine.'

The water was sucking out furiously now, and the tops of the rocks were just sticking up, glistening with water. I took a deep breath and leaped over to the first, my boot finding traction as I shifted my weight forwards and stepped on to the next rock. I knew my foot wouldn't hold – it was slipping across the wet surface – and I threw my arms out so that at least I would fall on to the rough rock of the gully's other side and not into the gushing water.

Harriet called my name, and I gritted my teeth as I hit the rock, my palms grazing across the barnacles and a sharp edge knocking my torso.

For a few seconds I was winded, but then I clambered to safety.

'I'm alright,' I shouted, looking across the gully at Harriet.

All the colour had drained from her face, and she was shaking her head.

'You can do it, Harriet!' I yelled. Now that I was across, a surge of excitement swept through me; my heart beat faster, and I felt wild with the proximity to danger, the risk. I laughed, and Harriet's eyebrows folded together in fear and frustration.

'I can't jump as far as you,' she called, the sound hard to make out above the rushing water.

'You can!'

My eyes flicked down to the mouth of the gully, the narrow opening where the water surged in and out, and I wondered whether a body would fit through that space and, if it did, how quickly it would be dragged under the forest of kelp and whether it would ever be found again.

'Kate – now?' she asked.

I scanned the gully and out past the break to see what was coming. There was not going to be a better chance.

'Go!' I shouted.

She jumped, wobbling already as she left the ledge. One foot down, a little splash as her boot hit the rock under the surface. Both of her arms stretched wide, her face pure determination. The leap to the second rock, her arms out and grasping for the same ledge I had crashed into. I held my breath. Then she was collapsing forwards, dress sodden at the bottom, hands reaching up to the ledge and to me.

I grabbed her shoulders and pulled her towards me as she scrambled the rest of the way up and away from the water. We stayed like that, my arms around her back, her face at my chest, breathing heavily, our legs tangled under us, our skirts wet and heavy.

She looked at me. 'I did it.' She laughed and grabbed my face with both her hands and kissed me, full on the mouth. Just for a moment.

She pulled away, eyes shining and hair wild, framing her face.

'I did it!' she yelled again, and threw her arms into the air and whooped with delight, while I sat staring at her, my body filled with the tingling strangeness of her kiss.

71

And this time it was Harriet who led us back across the rocks, jumping and leaping and calling for me to catch up, while I trailed behind, feeling as though something had burst open in both of us, wondrously, and yet it was not the same thing. As we made our way home, Harriet kept pulling further and further away from me.

THIRTEEN

I came down with a dreadful cold; the type where my face felt stuffed full of damp laundry rags. I could not breathe through my nose, and I snuffled and coughed and moped about until Mother ordered me to bed with a spoonful of Glover's mixture and a washer for my head and told me to stay put until I'd burned the thing away with a fever.

Ordinarily I might have relished an excuse to lie in bed and take one of Harriet's books from my shelf and read and reread the words that lifted me up and straight off the cape and away to adventure. But not even Ralph's adventures on the Coral Islands could pull me from my glumness. For today, I knew, McPhail was escorting all the children to watch the whales off the point at Murray's Beach, and I so dearly wanted to go. He had been fishing out there lately and had told Father that the whales were passing in large numbers, and he offered to take us all down there on an excursion of sorts.

When Harriet came to collect me and found me bed-ridden, I noticed a quiet triumph behind her concerned face, that she would go to the point with McPhail – she would exclaim as the whales breached and showed their secret skins to the sky and hold her hand to her chest and sigh – without me.

Of course I knew she would not be alone. She would have all the others with her, but they would be distracted and not notice the things that I might see.

Listening to the comings and goings from the kitchen I could hear when they were ready to leave, and I pushed back the blankets and went to the window.

Across the grass, I saw Harriet holding Sadie's reins while Emmaline stood behind her with a basket, a loaf of bread wrapped in a red and white cloth protruding from its side. Albert and James had obviously not deigned to go for I did not see them, but Will and Harry were there, and Lucy sat up on the horse with her arms wrapped around little Edward.

I drew the curtain across and sulked back to my bed.

The day passed so slowly. I tossed and turned, not feverish as much as agitated. I desperately wanted them all to return so that I might know what had transpired. Mother brought me tea and toast but then grew weary with my constant calling out to ask whether or not they were home.

'Kate, you'll never get better if you don't rest. Lie down, for goodness sake, and sleep!'

But I could not. And it was an endless few hours I spent picking up my book and throwing it aside again before I heard them coming back.

Finally Emmaline rushed in through our bedroom door.

'Where's Harriet?' I asked, as she strode past me to fling herself down on her bed.

'She had to go straight home – her mother said.'

Was that true? I thought about Harriet returning from the outing, then slipping away again down the track to meet McPhail where none of the younger ones could see.

'So, do you want to hear about it or not?' Emmaline's voice cut into my daydreaming.

'How many did you see?' I asked, even though I could not have cared less about the whales. Surely Emmaline realised this, but she went into great detail about the size and the shape of the pod and did not mention McPhail once.

'And did you all behave for Mr McPhail?' I asked.

'I did, if that's what you're asking,' she said impertinently.

'And how was Mr McPhail?' I was searching for some clue that I might stew over.

'I hardly saw him,' she said.

'Whatever do you mean, Emmaline? You went with the man.'

As much as she pretended that she wasn't, Emmaline was flattered by my interest in what she had to say.

'Well,' she said, stretching out the telling now that she had my attention. 'McPhail took Harriet off around the point where she would be able to see better, and Harriet told me and Will and Harry to stay with the little ones because it was too dangerous.'

So Harriet had made the most of my absence. I wondered if she had need of a hand to help her up the steep rocks, if she had stumbled a little and found herself falling into the strong arms of the man who accompanied her.

'And were they gone for long?'

Emmaline sat up on her bed. 'I can't remember. Gosh, I'm famished. When's dinner, do you think? I'm going to ask Mother.'

And she was off. I would have no more news from Emmaline now that her stomach had her attention. Which left me with my imagination, and that was a far more dangerous thing.

FOURTEEN

Soon enough I had other things to occupy my mind, as September came around and the preparations for Christmas, a grand affair at the lighthouse, began in earnest. Mother always did the pudding, and I helped as I grew older. But this year was to be the first she would let me make the pudding on my own. I was excited, and nervous.

The pudding was the centrepiece of Christmas dinner. Mother said it reminded her of her own mother, and her mother's mother before. I thought of all those women going back in time, making puddings for their families, passing down the recipe. It made me feel small, but anchored. Tied to a thing that went back further than I could imagine. Had any of them thought that sometime in a distant future a fifteen-year-old girl would use the recipe on a light station in Australia?

Mother, Emmaline and I were cutting biscuits from dough when my brothers' calls drifted in through the kitchen window.

'Boat's in!'

Mother wiped her hands on her apron. 'Let's see if Patterson managed to get my order right this year,' she said, and set the last tray of biscuits aside. 'Emmaline, get these in the oven and watch them. And don't you eat any! The captain will be wanting one with a hot cup of tea once we've got the supplies unpacked.'

'I want to go to the boat,' said Emmaline, crossing her arms.

'No, you're to stay here. Kate can come and help,' Mother

said, ushering me out the door. I smirked at Emmaline behind Mother's back, and she stuck out her tongue.

James and Will were scampering about on the jetty as the supply boat moved closer.

'Ahoy, Captain!' Will shouted. 'Got anything special for us today?'

'Indeed, I have,' Captain Patterson called from the prow as he drew alongside the jetty. 'You've gone and grown again, lads. What's your mother been feeding you for you to get so tall? You'll be taller than your sister by the next time I visit.'

He tipped his hat at Mother and me as we joined the boys on the jetty. 'Now, before you go asking, Mrs Gilbert, I've got some terrible news about your Christmas supplies.'

'Don't you go teasing me or I'll send you away without a single taste of the jam biscuits the girls have made you.'

'Oh no,' said Patterson, frowning theatrically. 'We can't have that.' He rummaged around the boxes and sacks on the deck until her found a cloth bag and passed it over the side to Mother. 'Here they are for you, Mrs Gilbert, as requested. Nothing's missing.'

Mother smiled. 'Come on then. Let's get this unpacked and we'll get the kettle on for you.'

By now Father and Walker had also appeared and were unloading the supplies. It was a thankless task, the moving of those packages up the track to the station. As always, James found the biggest, heaving it onto his scrawny shoulders and staggering a little under the weight.

'You'll never get that all the way up,' I scoffed.

James deliberately knocked into me as he went past. 'What would you know about hard work anyway, Kate? You're just a girl.'

I grabbed a sack of potatoes, bent my knees and pinned my elbows against my side as I tried to lift it to rest against my waist.

'Whoa there, miss!' called Patterson. 'Leave that one be – that's work for your father and brothers, that is.'

'Kate!' Mother said curtly. 'Just bring the mail.'

I took the small bag she held out to me and stomped up the path after my brothers. I hoped they choked on their jam biscuits.

That evening after Father and Patterson had retired to the parlour with a new bottle of whiskey, Mother assembled the ingredients for me on the broad bench in the kitchen. There were plump raisins, crystalline mixed peel, handfuls of sticky sultanas and clumped black currants. The bottle of brandy stood next to the sugar jar, a small brown paper packet of mixed spices, vanilla essence, and a lemon that mother had reverently taken from the sand-lined box where she kept the fruit wrapped to stop spoiling. Next to these, and arranged like a surgeon's instruments, were the wooden spoon that had been my mother's mother's, the biggest of our mixing bowls and the scales.

'Off you go then,' Mother said and nodded at the tattered recipe that sat amongst all this on the bench.

The handwriting of a grandmother I had never met told me the exact measurements I would need, the order in which I should do each task. Mother, of course, had no need for the recipe, and yet each year she pulled it from its place, tucked into her collection, and ran her fingers over the lines as though this act might return her mother to her.

I carefully shook the raisins onto the scales. The task of preparing the fruit was no more onerous than any number of recipes Mother churned out of that kitchen, yet there was a special ceremony to pudding making. The alchemic reaction of fruit and brandy and sugar, stirred once for each person we loved and prayed for. My mother's face always became drawn when she stirred for the ones we had lost; she'd cry for my brother then wipe her cheeks crossly, saying she'd spoil the mixture with tears.

Once I'd finished measuring all the quantities and placed them in the bowl, I added the brandy and mixed. The fruit was to bathe in the sweet spicy syrup of brandy and sugar for a month, during which time the bowl would sit majestically in the corner of the pantry covered in cloth. Some days I'd hear Mother murmuring as she bustled about in its presence, 'Let this be a good year, a healthy year; let us be blessed', and I wondered at the strange power the Christmas pudding had over us all.

A few days later I was checking on the fruit when I heard Mother come into the kitchen, accompanied by Mrs Walker and Mrs Jackson. I stayed where I was in the pantry, out of sight. I was not a sneak, but I did enjoy listening to the way these three women of the light station spoke to each other when they thought none of us children were around.

'You got the pudding started then, I suppose?' Mrs Walker said.

The kettle banged on the stove, and Mother replied. 'I'm glad to say it was Kate who prepared the fruit. I'm hoping she'll do it all this year.'

'Wish I had a girl as old as your two,' said Mrs Jackson. 'It's not the same with boys, and I've a few years before Lucy can be of any use in my kitchen.'

'Heaven knows they're not always a help!' Mrs Walker said.

'But your Harriet is a far sight more inclined to matters of the home and hearth than Kate is,' my mother said. 'If that girl had her way she'd spend all her days out on the rocks with one of those useless books your sister-in-law sends, Annie.'

Mrs Jackson's voice broke through the others. 'Well, rock hopping and books won't get her a husband, that's for sure.'

'Oh, I'm sure she'll grow out of it by then,' my mother said, but her voice had grown quieter.

'You'll need to make sure of it. Those girls – Harriet especially – they are close enough to marrying age now, and they should be behaving as such. I'll not have our Albert sweet on a girl who doesn't know her place.'

My eyebrows shot up in surprise.

'Albert's sweet on Harriet?' Mrs Walker asked, and laughed.

'On Kate,' Mrs Jackson replied, and my heart thumped wildly. 'He knows a beauty like Harriet wouldn't marry a boy like him.'

There was an uncomfortable silence, then Mrs Walker hurried to cover Mrs Jackson's rudeness. 'Kate will have suitors enough when it's her time – she's a beauty in her own way.'

'Enough of this,' Mother said. 'It's making me feel old to think of my daughter married off. Let's take the tea to the verandah and sit. It'll soon be time to start on dinner.'

I waited until they had gone and then I slipped out of the kitchen and into my room, where I could think more about what had been said. Albert – sweet on me! Was it true? And did it mean anything at all, if he only liked me because he thought Harriet out of reach?

FIFTEEN

There had been trouble with the light for a few nights. It was to do with the mantle and it had my father huffing and grumbling, and we knew well enough to steer clear of him until it had been righted. He had his books out on the kitchen table while Jackson did his shift, and he reckoned he had one more idea of how he might fix it; after that he'd have to send for a new part and it would be at least four or five days of all kinds of business to get our lighthouse to throw its steady light out to sea.

At first Mother tried soothing him with gentle words and the warm touch of her hand on his forearm, but she was stretched herself with getting ready for Christmas and she needed the table space.

Eventually she was short with him, and he stormed out into the night. Mother sighed and, despite the work ahead of her, took to baking to make peace.

By the time I'd finished washing up the dinner dishes, she had a currant pie hot in her hands, and the smell was pastry and egg and the sweet tang of currants all wound into one, steaming and delicious.

'Kate, would you be a dear and take this up to your father? I'm dead on my feet.'

'The whole thing? Don't we get to have some?'

'If you nip up quick you might be lucky enough to get a piece from your father.'

That night there was little wind, a strange thing on our cape, and it was clear and moonless. Out the door of the cottage I had to stop to look up, the pie dish warm through the cloth in my hands. Studding the indigo sky were thousands and thousands of stars. On nights like this, you could almost feel the planet moving on its axis.

During the blue and sunny days, one could choose to forget our place in the universe, the fact of the planets, the complicated trickery of the earth spinning in place and coming around each day anew to face the sun, to face the moon. I must admit to being incredulous when Mr Jamieson first taught us about the universe. I turned, smirking, to Harriet to roll my eyes at what I thought was all a tremendous hoax to catch us out and teach us the importance of listening, or not believing fairytales or other nonsense.

But I came to believe in Mr Jamieson's strange account and, on nights like this, it made so much sense: to see the vastness of the night sky and consider the endless possibilities. In my mind I tried to fathom what Mr Jamieson had said: that when we looked up at the stars, we were gazing into the past. Pinpoints of light in the darkness, so quiet and still, breathing not a word of what the future held for us.

Remembering my errand, I hurried to the lighthouse and ran up the steps to the light. As I approached the underbelly of the tower, the heat of the pie pan seeped through the cloth in my hands and I raced up the metal rungs of the short ladder.

I steadied myself as I came through the trapdoor into the tower, the pie thrust out before me as my offering.

'Mother's made you a currant pie.'

Father lifted his head from where he leaned over the bench next to Jackson, and his face seemed to soften. 'There's a good girl. Put it over here – I'll make some room.'

As Father went to move some papers for me, I noticed that Albert was standing behind Jackson. The heat from my palms seemed to travel all over me. All I could think of was what I had been mulling over this past week, what I'd heard that day in the pantry. I wasn't sure where to look when he straightened up and nodded his head at me.

I lowered my eyes to the speckled top of the pie. I tried to inch around him to place the dish on the cleared bench, but the space was small and I could not help my skirts brushing against the back of Albert's legs.

We both shifted hastily away from each other.

'This'll be the last time we'll try it, boys,' my father said. 'I need you fresh for your shift tomorrow, Jackson. But a slice of pie will do nicely before we try switching it over again.'

I knew Father kept some kitchen utensils in his bench and I busied myself with working out which drawer held the knife. I pulled the smooth wooden knobs and slid the drawers in and out, seeing papers and ink and pen nibs and string, before I found the one with a spoon, and the long silver blade of a knife.

I sensed Albert come up beside me at the bench as I sliced thick triangles of the pie and wished that Father had some plates so that I might serve with some decorum.

'That looks delicious,' Albert said.

I relaxed a little. He did not know what I had heard from the pantry; he was not behaving awkwardly.

'It's Father's favourite. I guess Mother thought he deserved it, since he's been working so hard.'

'A good wife,' Albert said and nodded as if he were older and wiser than I knew him to be. I suddenly had the urge to pinch him low on his hip, where his shirt met his pants, and tell him he sounded ridiculous.

I offered him the pie pan, turning the cut pieces towards him. Father and Jackson also took slices but hardly glanced up from what they were poring over.

I hesitated, unsure whether I should take a piece for myself and, if I did, whether I should stand or sit. When Father and I were alone up here together, I felt at home, and as though I joined in the reign over the darkness and the black sea. But the presence of Albert and his father interrupted that, and I felt childish, as though this were a place I ought not to be.

Father must have sensed me hovering there. 'Albert,' he said, 'will you see Kate back down the tower?'

Albert wiped his hands on his pants and nodded.

'Take the rest of the pie back for you and your mother and the other children for tomorrow,' Father said. 'You're a good girl for bringing it up. Tell your mother she's heaven-sent.'

'There's no need for Albert to see me down, Father. I'll be fine. I always am.'

The kettle would be on the hearth in the kitchen, and I would eat my pie with a cup of tea; Mother might still be up.

'It's time you were both in bed,' Father said. 'If it pains you to think you are being escorted, my dear, then consider that you are both accompanying each other.' He left it at that and raised one eyebrow at Jackson as they bent back down over their work.

I saw Jackson smile.

Albert was staring at his feet, chewing the last of his pie, and the corner of his mouth was curling up. They were all laughing at me.

'Fine. Keep up!' I started down the stairs.

I heard my father snort and then the shuffle of Albert's feet across the timber, but I was already clanging down the ladder and onto the spiral staircase. My feet knew its rhythm and length, but I had to keep my wits about me to move so fast.

The stairwell was dark, and lit only every few turns by lanterns embedded in the thick walls. The noise of our footsteps echoed as Albert gained on me. His steps were louder and less rhythmic, but they were quick.

'Keep up, you say?' He was behind me now, only a few paces back.

My neck tensed, as it did when Harriet and I played scary games in the dark, imagining ghosts and terrible demons creeping over the sea-cliffs to drag young girls from the cape back down to their watery world. I let out a little squeak and rushed to go faster, my breathing more frantic now and my blood pumping in my ears.

We were approaching the bottom; I could see the whitewashed floor glowing faintly beyond the next curl of iron.

'You're not that fast, Kate Gilbert.' Albert was on the step behind me now, and could easily have overtaken me if he wanted, but instead he stayed there, urging me on.

We spiralled down around that last bend, and I leaped off the bottom step to rush out towards the open door and the path, the grass beyond. But a hand stretched out clumsily, grabbing at my waist, so that I was pulled around to face him.

'Got you,' he said, and I felt light and alive and prickling, as if there were salt drying on my skin after swimming in the sea.

'You did.' I placed my hand on his and removed it from my waist. 'Good night, Albert,' I said, and moved away because I wasn't at all sure what it was my body was doing and whether I liked it or was afraid.

SIXTEEN

It was Blackwell who alerted us. He came pounding on the door of our cottage early one morning a few weeks later.

'Mr Gilbert,' he called, and banged again on the door.

'Whatever is it?' Father grumbled, pushing his chair back from the table and setting down his tea, which I knew he hated to have interrupted. He strode down the hall to greet Blackwell and find out what the urgent matter was.

Turned out it was a whale. One of the last of the season. A female had near beached herself on the rocks at Murray's, and the tide was on the turn so she'd surely be stuck by mid morning and what else could we do, said Blackwell, but cut her up on the spot and quick before the oil leaked or the blubber fouled.

I came up behind Father to listen to the man explain himself, and my hand flew to my mouth at his suggestion. I was not the kind of girl who was queasy at the thought of blood – far from it – but to slaughter a beast as magnificent as a whale ourselves? We could not.

I knew that there were fortunes being made by those who chased and killed the whales. I knew that light stations all up and down the coast still depended on their stinking oil for fuel, but I could not bear the thought of a creature so big being brought down by a man, especially a man such as Blackwell.

My father evidently didn't think any immediate action was

necessary, for he said, 'Might she not strike out again for the open water when the tide is high this afternoon?'

Blackwell stroked his greasy beard. 'She might, for sure, Mr Gilbert. But then we'd have lost what might have made us a pretty penny.'

Father's mouth creased, revealing his discomfort. He knew that the killing of a whale – with the blubber to be rendered into oil, the bone itself – would make a handy increase in our yearly income. If we got to the meat before it spoiled, there would be that, too. We had heard, in the past, of men up the coast learning off the blacks how to make the most of a stranded whale. Money aside, the thought still turned my stomach and, from the look of it, my father's also.

'If you don't want to be part of it I'll get some men from Bennett's to help me carve her up. But then we could do with the lend of a horse and a wagon, Mr Gilbert, to get the blubber up to Edenstown so as to be rendered down – the whalebone as well. There's enough for us all to share in the spoils.'

Father thought for a minute. 'Murray's, you say. I'll follow you down, Blackwell, to see what might be done.'

He fetched his oilskin, and Blackwell leaned back against the verandah post and brought a pipe from out of his pocket.

I was bursting to tell Harriet the dreadful news, but I would have to get past Blackwell to do it. I gathered myself and stepped on to the verandah, keeping my eyes averted lest he catch my gaze.

'You and yer friend should come down and see the beast,' he murmured, low enough for me to hear, but not for Father to.

I ignored him.

'Will be quite a show when we stick her and bleed her.'

I swept past him, as though I didn't care at all what he said, and ran for Harriet's cottage.

By late morning, there was a little crowd assembled down on Murray's Beach. Blackwell and Father and Walker, the older boys – Albert, James, Will and Harry – and Harriet and me.

As we'd rounded the track we'd seen another figure on the beach who had beaten us there. From his tall silhouette, I knew at once it was McPhail. By the tightening of Harriet's hand in mine, it was clear she knew it, too.

Beyond McPhail was the whale. It was lying in the craggy space made between two rock ridges, and water was pushing up and over its bulk each time a set of waves came in. The blue-grey hide of it glistened in the sun, and it looked so unearthly there, pulled up from the deep and deposited on land where it should not rightly go. Oh, it made me sad to see it.

'Look, Kate – over there!' Harriet pointed out to sea, and I saw the last falling shower of a whale's plume and, breaking the surface of the water, there was the same arc of whale skin, a smaller beast than this one.

'It must be the calf,' I said, my chest strangely heavy. 'Come for its mother.'

Father had noticed our pointing and directed his gaze out at the calf. McPhail walked over to join him on the hard sand, where the tide was steadily retreating, and neither of them turned when Blackwell came to stand beside them.

Father said that if the whale didn't loose itself and head back out to sea with the afternoon tide then Blackwell could have his wish. Blackwell looked pleased and set off to Bennett's River to collect some men and some tools.

Harriet and I crossed our fingers, two sets each, that the whale would hear its calf's mournful calls and also that this would be enough, when the water surged high and fast, to pull the whale back to the open ocean and let it on its way.

And so we waited. It passed lunchtime, and Harriet and I handed around the oat biscuits and cordial that we had packed. We two ate perched on separate rocks, each with a view to the whale. The boys raced around, playing at being pirates, darting in towards the whale and hightailing it away again when Father called for them to keep clear.

At some point, Harriet asked, 'Might I touch it?'

'Best to stay back,' Father replied. 'It's a big beast and still alive, and with the water coming in again, we wouldn't want you crushed.'

'Oh,' said Harriet.

It was always hard for those who disappointed Harriet, because her pretty face fell in such a manner that one felt as though they had dealt her the gravest blow. Inevitably whoever had disappointed her about-turned on their decision. Harriet knew this, of course, and used it to her advantage.

This time, however, Father was distracted by the rising waves, and it was McPhail who saw her fallen face.

'I see no reason why you couldn't, if someone stands beside you to keep you safe,' he said.

I noticed then the frank look she gave him as her eyes met his. I shifted my gaze quickly for it seemed as if I had witnessed something I shouldn't have. It thrilled me, that look, but it twisted inside me that I had neither given nor received anything like it.

'Thank you, Mr McPhail,' Harriet said, and I stood up to go with her for she had voiced what I'd been wishing, too. What it might be like to run a hand down that great blue flank, what it might feel like under my skin.

'One at a time, I think best,' said Harriet.

Of course, it occurred to me: this is what she had intended all along – to get a moment to be close to McPhail, just the two of them.

Father, I could see, thought nothing of it and nodded as though it were a good suggestion after all. I did notice, though, that Walker watched closely as his daughter stepped from rock to rock, leaning into the tall body of the man next to her.

When Harriet and McPhail reached the great head of the whale, Harriet removed her right hand from McPhail's forearm to splay her fingers against the blue-grey hide. McPhail moved in near to Harriet, to the whale, and brought up his left hand and placed it next to hers so that they were joined by the edge of skin on their littlest fingers.

I could not have looked away had I wanted to. The air around the whale appeared to quiver slightly and then a plume of spray burst from the top of the whale's head, and Harriet leaped away. McPhail's arm shot out to grab her waist and they stumbled back together.

Harriet turned to him then, still gripped in his arm, and she tipped her head back and laughed, and McPhail smiled at her, a great splitting of his face, so that it was as if I were seeing that expression for the first time, as if I were seeing the boy McPhail. There were his teeth, the foreign curve of his cheek. And then, as sudden as it had come, the moment ended, and they moved apart from one another.

Harriet looked at me triumphantly before noticing her father's alert, steady gaze.

'Watch out!' Father called as a high wave curled up, and we all scattered.

By the time Blackwell and his ragged crew arrived from Bennett's River with their saws and hammers and ropes, the tide was sloshing all the way in around the whale's head and, every time a wave surged in, she raised her great tail and brought it down with a heavy splash.

Harriet returned to my side and, although I tried to be distant, eventually we huddled together on a rock, quietly cheering and clapping our hands together as the water rose higher and the whale became more active.

Out in the bay, the calf emerged from the waves every so often.

'Poor thing,' said Harriet. 'How awful it would be. Knowing its mother is stuck here and there's not a thing it can do to help.' She stretched her legs out in front of her, revealing her little black boots and stockings, and she tilted her ankles so her feet swung from side to side. 'I wouldn't know what to do at all if I had to get on without Mother. Though I suppose one day I must. But I really can't bear to think of it at all. Can you?'

Harriet had been spared the intimacy I'd already had with

grief and loss. No doubt it was hard for her mother to have endured the loss of a baby and the certainty that she would never have another besides Harriet. But that could not be as difficult as having a child, raising him and losing him, as my mother had done, and as all our family had done with her in our own ways.

'No, I do not like to think of it either,' I said as I stood and shielded my eyes.

The men were gathering closer to the whale, and there were raised voices.

'Come,' I said to Harriet and motioned with my hand for her to follow.

Blackwell was standing next to my father and gesturing at the whale.

'We wait any longer and she'll move off – we'll lose any chance,' Blackwell said.

The men gathered behind him murmured in agreement.

Father looked troubled. I knew it pained him to see the great whale stuck against the rocks, so undignified. He was a light keeper: it was his duty to see the citizens of the sea safely past the cape, and the imminent destruction of the whale seemed to be against every tenet of his profession. But there was no ignoring the truth of what Blackwell said. Father would be denying the other men income, a windfall really, if he continued to hold back the group gathered there.

But hold them back he did – that was the truth of it. No matter that he had no real position of authority over them, my father presided over the cape and his word was as good as rule. But there was a brittleness to the air around Father and Blackwell, as though Blackwell might at any moment determine that Father had no right at all to tell him what he could and could not do.

I glanced at McPhail to see whether he might support my father, but he did not seem to care one way or another if the whale lived or died. He was a fisherman. He baited and hooked and took his catch, the same as the others. If the bounty of the sea was going to throw itself up on the shores, who was he to refuse it?

The whale used the next set of waves to thump her tail, and we all stared. Harriet's hand flew out and gripped my wrist, and we watched in awe as the water gushed in and around the whale and her huge head lifted a little from where it was resting in the rocks and ever so slightly she slid backwards a foot, maybe, at most.

'Fer Christ's sake!' cursed Blackwell, and he moved towards the whale.

But my Father called 'Wait!' and held out his arm to block Blackwell's path.

And in that moment the water rushed in, and the whale pushed and lifted and slid out from her holding place into the waves. She listed there for a few seconds so that we saw the ridged pale skin of her belly before she went down and under, and headed out to her calf.

Harriet and I jumped in the air and cheered. We wrapped our arms around each other.

'Hoorah, hoorah!' we yelled – for the whale, for the getting away.

SEVENTEEN

By the time we all made it back up the track to the station, it was time for dinner.

Mother and Emmaline had spent the whole day baking pies. I suspected that swimming in the gravy were more potatoes and flour than meat, as the lamb stocks were running low, but what did it matter when the pies sat in the centre of the table, all golden pastry and steam curling from the slits in the top? There were four of them to be sliced and shared, and some carrots and mash to go alongside. Mother had not been sure of how many might come back to eat, so she and I hastily set up a table in the kitchen for the younger children and then pulled in some chairs from the verandah so we could all crowd around.

We ate with gusto. Blackwell's behaviour on the beach had not stopped him from availing himself of a free meal at our table. He ate with an aggrieved churlishness.

I nudged Harriet, who sat beside me. 'Look at him,' I whispered. 'What a brute.'

'Shush, Kate,' she said, and smothered a giggle in her napkin. Her cheeks were flushed, and she seemed to be bursting with all the emotion of the day.

Father sat back in his chair and declared that it was the tastiest meal he had shared in some time, and that Mother and Emmaline had done themselves proud.

'Let us share in each other's company a little longer,' he said. 'Shall we sing?'

'Oh yes, let's!' cried Harriet for she, of course, had the sweetest voice of any of us.

We retired to the sitting room, which Mother hurried to make habitable. She asked me to fetch a bottle of sherry and the small glasses from the cabinet, and I placed them on a tray on the sideboard and offered round the glasses to the men.

Father told the children to run off and play or sit and listen, and it was only little Lucy and Albert who joined the party in the end.

'Well, then, Harriet, a song if you will?' said Father.

Blackwell muttered, and while I could not hear the words, I guessed at their meaning. I glared at him.

Harriet lowered her eyes as was proper, I suppose, in showing a degree of modesty about the whole affair, but at her mother's urging she went to sit at the piano. Mrs Walker had tried to teach us both when we were younger, but Harriet had the greater propensity. I, on the other hand, was all thumbs and could neither master the black and white keys before me, nor the complicated sheets of music; they would not speak to me like the lines of text I raced through in books.

Harriet settled herself on the piano stool and lifted her hands to the keys. The piano was in a poor condition generally – it was too expensive to get someone out to tune it. We tended to make do by covering the clanking discordant notes with hearty singing whenever we had such an evening.

Harriet's wrists were long and slender with the neat button of her sleeve pulled back a little so she might play. With all eyes on her, I was free to observe her as the others did, and she seemed somehow distant from me. Her face, the very shape of her, were so familiar to me, and yet, tonight, in the lantern light in that crowded room, she was no longer only mine.

She lifted her fingers and played a chord, a pleasing one, and then her voice rang out.

My Bonnie lies over the ocean
My Bonnie lies over the sea
My Bonnie lies over the ocean
O bring back my Bonnie to me …

It truly was a sweet voice, and I saw Father close his eyes and smile at the verse. Mrs Walker nodded her head gently.

Harriet played another single chord, and inclined her head to us to indicate we should accompany her. Slowly, quietly at first, a few voices joined hers.

I hated singing in front of others, for I knew my voice was awful. Albert had come to stand beside me, and I moved away slightly so that he would not hear how tuneless I was.

Bring back, bring back
O bring back my Bonnie to me, to me
Bring back, bring back
O bring back my Bonnie to me.

I felt a nudge in my ribs. Albert grinned at me.

'Don't you laugh at me,' I admonished him.

'I'm not,' he whispered back.

'Harriet is the songstress – not me.'

'I don't care much for singing,' he said softly, and the next chord on the piano vibrated right at the core of me. A strange feeling, not unwelcome at all.

I stared straight ahead but I knew he was watching me.

Harriet's voice rang out even stronger now, and I chanced a look at McPhail as she went into the next verse. He was standing against the mantle over the fireplace but he could not keep his eyes from Harriet. They were filled, I saw, with a kind of longing. Albert looked at me with tenderness sometimes, but it was nothing like the desperation in McPhail's gaze.

I forced myself to glance away and, as I did, I caught the eye of Mrs Walker, who traced back to where my attention had been. I witnessed her puzzlement at McPhail's expression, and the way her face moved to a sudden understanding as she looked from him to Harriet and back again.

O blow the winds o'er the ocean,
And blow the winds o'er the sea
O blow the winds o'er the ocean
And bring back my Bonnie to me.

We all joined her to sing the final chorus, but I was rigid now with nerves. It was as though I were approaching the climactic scene in a book, and I wanted to read on and also I didn't, for once I went on, I would know what happened and all the possibilities and imaginings would be reduced to one ending.

I almost wanted Mrs Walker to cause a scene. But then, as always, I was entrapped by my love, my loyalty for Harriet, and I wanted to warn her, to beseech McPhail to look away, for goodness sake. The haunted, hungry look in his eyes had now gone and in its place were tears, which he roughly wiped away.

Harriet stood up and moved back from the piano and we all clapped. Soon after, the evening ended and our guests left. It turned out, however, that Harriet's fate had been sealed.

As we were finishing dinner a few days later, our door burst open and Harriet appeared, wild and breathless.

'Whatever's the matter, Harriet?' I said, and appealed to Mother with my eyes.

'You can leave the table, dear,' she said.

I suspect, thinking back on it, that she already knew exactly what Harriet was about to reveal to me.

'I am being sent to Melbourne!' Harriet said, clutching both my hands in hers, once we were sat on my bed.

'You're what?'

'Melbourne. They are sending me to Melbourne to stay with Aunt Cecilia for three months. Three whole months! I am so desperately excited but I told Mother that I could not go without you. Melbourne – can you imagine! And I will stay at Aunt Cecilia's grand house and be introduced around and may have suitors.'

My head was spinning. Not once had I considered that this would be the outcome of that night.

'But when will you go?'

'After Christmas, January sometime. I am overwhelmed at the thought of it, Kate! But I told Mother I could not go without you.'

'And what did she say?' I said, already knowing the answer.

Harriet bowed her head and was quiet. 'She said it was not possible.' She gripped my fingers tighter in hers. 'She said that Aunt Cecilia could not be expected to be responsible for two young ladies, and that your mother could not do without you here, that it would not be fair.'

Oh, the hurt of it. The furious envy that bloomed in me. Harriet would go to Melbourne! I knew that this possibility had been spoken of but I never really imagined it would happen. That Harriet would go away. Away from the cape, to adventures unknown and new sights and new places and the types of things I read about and dreamed about and lay awake wondering about. That Harriet should go and not I? That she could win that look from McPhail *and* get to go to Melbourne? I could have roared.

My indignity rose higher in my throat until all I could do was let out a strangled, 'No. No, it would not be fair to Mother. In fact I must go back and help clear the dishes.' And I rushed from the room so that she wouldn't see my tears.

I heard her call after me, but she knew well enough to leave me be. I hid in the darkness of the verandah and watched her walk slowly back to her cottage, curling my fingers tight into a fist that I bit so that no one would hear my sobs.

And the next day, despite Harriet's news, life went on as before. I was glad for Harriet, truly I was, and I lay with her in the sun as she planned and chatted.

As Christmas approached, she grew ever more impatient for Melbourne and then would turn and cry and say she could never leave. I took the tears; I took the embraces; I took the wailing. I joined in all of it. For I loved her – I loved her, and I wished her well.

EIGHTEEN

Then Christmas was upon us. Harriet and I loved the occasion and always made each other a special gift. When we were younger, it might have been a tiny doll created from shells, or a picture we'd drawn, framed in some old fencing. Once I gave Harriet a story I'd written about two princesses who had been secretly stowed away on an isolated cape when they were babies so that they would not be harmed before they could take their rightful place as Queens of their lands.

That morning I had given Harriet a handkerchief I had stitched with our initials intertwined in vivid indigo cotton on one corner. It had taken me an age to get the tiny stitches right, and Mother had helped me with the design, a green vine curling around the straight lines, dotted with tiny yellow flowers, like those that spotted our cape come the spring.

'So you don't forget us while you are away,' I said as she unwrapped it.

'Never,' Harriet said. 'I love it.' She examined the needlework and ran her finger across the monogram. 'I will keep it forever.'

I could not help blushing with pleasure, her approval and delight the best presents I would receive that day.

We often had guests come Christmas time, and we always invited the men from Bennett's River who worked for us periodically, and more often than not others showed up who knew they would not be turned away on such a day. Father would be jolly and benevolent, a gracious host, though in truth it was Mother who did all the work.

I was in the hot and bustling kitchen, worrying about how the pudding would turn out, when I heard a cough at the back kitchen door. It was McPhail. He carried a long sack, clutched in both hands. I took my handkerchief from my apron pocket and pressed it against my forehead.

'I've brought your mother a salmon. She's probably got enough but this one's a beauty. I pulled her in this morning.'

I took the bag from him and peered into it. The silvery snout of the fish pointed up, one glossy eye appearing to fix on me.

'Mother will appreciate it.' I held the bag out in front of me, not wanting the fishy wetness of it to seep into my apron and skirt, but not wanting to appear rude.

'Go and find yourself a seat,' Mother called to him from behind me. 'You're just in time.'

McPhail dipped his head and moved away.

'Kate! The potatoes! And that gravy'll need a stir.'

I turned back to the flurry of the kitchen, the air thick with the smell of roasting meat and the rich undernote of the pudding, boiling away in readiness for its unveiling.

'Put it away over there by the sink, Kate. We'll do it for supper.' Under her breath Mother added, 'As if I've got time to deal with salmon now …' She continued her mumbling as she sliced the enormous hunk of beef in front of her.

I tried to smooth my hair back before I went out to take my place at the long table we'd set on the verandah, with the younger children crowded around one end. I noticed that McPhail sat next to Jackson, down and across from Harriet and me, while Albert slid in beside me.

'Merry Christmas, Kate,' he said.

'And to you, Albert.' I smiled, tapping my glass of lemonade against his.

'You've done a fine job of the dinner.'

'Wait till you see the pudding. Mother let me do it myself.'

'Then I'll look forwards to it all the more. You're quite the cook, I hear.' Albert ducked his head down as he paid the compliment.

A quiet warmth spread through me.

We were all dressed up for the occasion, buttoned up and laced in. Harriet was wearing a teal-and-white-striped taffeta dress with a cameo brooch at her throat. Her hair fell in golden curls around her face, and she did not look as if she belonged to this outpost, but as though she were already in Melbourne.

In the middle of our feast a great piece of honeycomb oozed, dark and sticky, onto a green china plate. James and Will had risked stings and broken limbs climbing to a fork of a big tree to steal the piece for Mother to add to the Christmas table. Now the plate took pride of place next to her willow-pattern platter piled high with the meat.

Harriet asked me to pass her some honeycomb, and I cut us both a piece. The knife cracked and stuck in the sticky hexagonal vessels, but I managed to carve out two wedges. I slid one piece onto my plate and passed the dish to Harriet.

She giggled as she picked up her piece, cupping one hand beneath the other as she attempted to move the sticky mess across to her plate. Honey dripped down her wrist and into the ruffle of her sleeve. McPhail was talking in earnest with Jackson, but I noticed him look up at the sound of Harriet's laugh. He carried on his conversation, but his eyes shifted from Jackson to Harriet and back again.

Harriet was well versed in table manners and etiquette and would often chastise me for my slovenly ways around guests or for my unladylike behaviour in general. I was surprised, then, when she lifted her hand to her mouth and her pink tongue darted out to lick the honey from the inside of her wrist. She only did it once, her lips and teeth resting softly on her skin while her tongue moved over the slick of honey. Across the table, McPhail picked up his glass and took a long swig of ale.

Harriet dropped her arm to her lap and exclaimed, 'Isn't it heavenly?'

'Delicious.'

'I wonder if they have it every day in Melbourne?' she said.

I wanted to say, *It's Christmas Day, Harriet. Can we not have one day where we do not speak of your Melbourne?* But I swallowed my bitterness and smiled. 'You will find out, no doubt.'

The eating and drinking rolled on with much toasting and laughter until everyone began to lean back in their chairs.

'Kate,' my mother said. 'Time to prepare the pudding.'

I rose importantly, enjoying the murmurs and gladness that spread around the table, and hurried into the kitchen.

Mother and Mrs Walker and Mrs Jackson bustled in and out, stacking plates and piling dishes. Harriet and Emmaline helped, too, ferrying jugs of custard and cream to the cleared table, as the din from the verandah grew louder.

There were sounds of scraping chairs as everyone moved away from the table, free to wander and talk before the dessert was brought out.

With Mother beside me, I grasped the long ends of calico that cradled the pudding bowl in the boiling water of the pot. Mother lifted the lid and clouds of steam billowed up.

'Watch your face, Kate. Slowly now.'

She took hold of the loose ends of the crossed calico, and we carefully lifted the pudding from its boiling bath. The scent of it, all brandy and fruit and butter, hung in those clouds of steam, and I knew my face was sweaty and red but I couldn't have been more pleased. I could prove myself in the domestic sphere, too. All the complaints of my wildness, my untameable nature; well, see here, everyone: Kate Gilbert – pudding maker.

I upended the pudding bowl onto a dish, and Mother and I held our breath as I tap, tap, tapped the bottom of the bowl, relishing the heavy thud of the pudding as it came loose. I lifted the bowl, and there it was, studded with glistening fruit, and the deep brown of butter, sugar and eggs cooked lovingly.

102

Mother put her arm around my waist and pulled me close. 'Well done, Kate. It's perfect.' I straightened my shoulders. 'Ready?' she asked.

I picked up the dish and followed her.

'Let's all take a seat now,' I heard her call from in front of me, followed by laughter and a few cheers as everyone returned to their seats.

The dish was heavy in my hands. As I came through the door, I saw Harriet smiling and clasping her hands together, then Albert's eyes, so clearly on me and not on the pudding; my father standing and proudly clapping. When I looked for McPhail, I found that he was not turned to me, as all the rest were, but faced across the table towards Harriet.

The afternoon light, so bright, blazed behind them all, catching the ends of their hair, Harriet's a golden halo around her face. *Like honey,* I was thinking, as my toe caught on an uneven board, as I tried desperately to shift the weight of the dish back in towards me, as I saw Mother reaching out for me.

I lurched forwards, the pudding sliding, sliding over the lip of the dish and smashing across the floor, the dish flipping after it and cracking in two as it hit the boards. I landed hard on my knees, one hand out in front of me, and I stayed there, staring at the mess of pudding and china before me.

There was a hush and then Father, my dear father, trying to salvage my honour with a joke, 'That's just how I like mine, Kate. Come on, everyone, serve yourself!'

'Oh, Tom,' my mother said softly.

My tears arrived then, stinging and unstoppable. There was a searing heat in my throat. I scrambled up and ran back into the kitchen, redolent with the smell of my broken pudding, and out the back door. Out and away to where I could hide and nurse my shame.

I couldn't bear the thought of seeing a single one of those faces ever again.

NINETEEN

It was Albert who found me. Harriet knew well enough to leave me alone with my hurt until I was good and ready to be seen again. She knew that I would be like a wounded animal, growling at anyone who was silly enough to come close, and that to intrude on my private humiliation was to make it more real – pity would only make it all the more profound.

But Albert knew none of this, only that he wanted to comfort me, his friend, his imagined sweetheart.

I had hidden away under a rocky overhang, on a narrow ledge that perched over the cliff to the side of the lighthouse. It wasn't far, but it was out of sight of anyone on land. I thought only the seabirds and the sailors could see me hunkering down there.

When I heard my name being called, I stayed silent as I didn't want him finding me there, hiding from everyone like the sulking child I was. Not long ago I had thought myself so grown up, so important, and now I had shamed myself in front of so many.

Albert was persistent and, before long, I heard him sliding nearby, a stream of pebbles and dust dislodging and clinking down the cliff face until they disappeared from view.

'There you are,' he said.

'Go away.'

I turned my head as far from him as possible, but he made

no move to leave. He shuffled into a sitting position and stayed quiet.

In fact, he remained so quiet that eventually I looked sideways to check that he was still there.

He had his knees pulled up against his chest and his wrists locked loosely in front of his shins. His eyes were fixed out to sea. I let my chin sink back into my hands, cupped on my knees, and stared out across the brilliant blue myself.

There was a breeze, and white caps peaked up here and there, white on blue. Thin streamers of cloud stretched across the sky. The sound of the sea was constant, but I never noticed it unless I really looked at the waves. Then I would hear the pulsing rhythm of it, a quiet roar, as familiar as my blood pumping through my veins.

I resented Albert for having found my hiding place yet his presence was somewhat comforting. Knowing that he wanted nothing from me, no outburst or tears or thanks, I could just sit and let the humiliation find its place amongst all the rest of me.

It would take many weeks before I stopped burning red in the face when I thought about the trip, the moment before it all smashed to pieces, and my grin, so pleased with myself. But, sitting on that ledge with Albert, I realised that the waves would keep pounding in, and no matter what I did, no matter how small or how great I thought my actions to be, they hardly mattered at all.

Albert's voice broke into our quiet. 'Two summers back I was playing with Harry down there on the rocks, and he slipped and fell.'

I shifted a little but said nothing.

'His foot hit a patch of seaweed and his legs went from under him. He fell straight down into the water. The tide was low, but the hole we were playing in was deep and waves were coming in against the rocks. In a second he was in and under, and I just stood there, frozen – I couldn't move. I thought he was gone.'

I waited for him to go on. When he did, his voice was quiet and tight.

'Finally I did go to the edge and looked down and there he was, drenched through, gripping on to the rock face for dear life. Not crying. I reached out to him and he held my arm as he climbed back up the rock. He would have made it on his own though, I reckon. He was so determined. I felt sick as we walked back up to the cottage; I knew the lashing that Mother would give me for not protecting one of her boys. I was such a coward, not jumping in after him. When we returned she was hanging sheets on the line and, as we got closer, she saw that Harry was soaked through. She said, "What the devil ..." and rushed towards us and demanded to know what had happened. And I went to tell, but it was Harry who spoke first.

'"I slipped and fell in. Albert pulled me out," he said, and I was silent and let him tell it that way. She hugged Harry and reached out her other hand to squeeze my arm.

'Harry never said anything to me about it. Maybe he didn't even mean to save my skin. Maybe that's how he remembers it. That was his story. It didn't seem to affect him and the next day he was dancing about the rocks again as if nothing ever happened. But me, well, I felt I'd been tested and found out – found to be a coward. I still think about it.' He stopped.

I'd never heard him speak for so long and wasn't sure why he'd told me all this. But if he'd intended to make me feel a little less awful, then it worked. My mind had been distracted from my own troubles by his story and, when I returned to my shame, I found it not as acute as I'd left it.

'I'm going to head back. They said there'd be beef sandwiches and a fish for tea. Will you come?' Albert said, and stood up.

I realised there was no reason not to slide along the ledge after him. He offered his hand to help me scramble up and, although I absolutely did not need it, I thought of his story and that stretched sound in his voice and took it. It was warm and rough and so much bigger than mine, and I clambered up after him. When I pulled my hand away and walked beside him back to the lighthouse, I could still feel the shape of it on my palm.

TWENTY

After Christmas a dense heat fell upon us, a heat without breeze, without relief. Night after night, Mother threw open all the windows, waving her arms as though to beckon the cooler night air into our home but, even then, we sweltered and sweated. Harriet and I counted down the days until she was to leave, and the memory of the pudding disaster slowly faded.

In recognition of our forthcoming separation, Mother and Mrs Walker lightened our house duties and often brought lunch down to us where we swam with all the children in the rock pools at the base of the cliff. With no wind at all, the sea hardly rippled, and we could see clear to the bottom of pools that were usually fizzing and frothy with foam.

At the lowest tide, just before lunchtime, all of us swam in the big pool that formed, jumping off the rocks to see who could make the biggest splash, holding our breaths and opening our eyes under water to watch the coloured fish, the spotted sea stars.

One day, even Father and Walker joined us, leaving Jackson to duties on the light. I imagined the poor crayfish at the bottom of the pool, scuttling away from this sudden influx of pale longer legs.

Harriet and I lolled in the water and out of it. We warmed ourselves on the rocks for a few minutes and then plunged back into the pool. Albert and James tried to chase us, but we screamed and dove away.

We had been in so long our fingers had crinkled, and I ran these strange new fingertips down Harriet's back, pretending I was a monster of the deep. She laughed and swam away from me.

Mother called lunch, entreating us all to get out for long enough to fill our bellies with some sustenance. Even though she demanded this, there was a relaxed note in her voice, as though she knew we would take our own sweet time and she might sit there a little longer, her bare feet in the water, her skirt bunched up around her calves.

So content was I, floating on my back and diving under to follow Harriet, that I didn't notice the two men coming down over the rocks.

The first I knew was Father calling out 'What's happened?' as he dried himself off on the edge of the rock. He put his shirt back on and strode off to meet the men: Jackson and McPhail.

Harriet and I stayed in the water and watched. We saw Walker hurry after Father, and Mother stood, covering her legs and raising a hand above her brow to block out the sun.

'What is it, Mother? What's wrong?' I asked.

But she was focused on the approaching men. Father reached them, and they stood clustered together. Jackson was speaking in earnest to Father while McPhail stood back a little, his arms crossed.

Harriet and I swam to the edge, leaving the other children to continue their play, and clambered up and onto the rock. On tiptoes we rock-hopped around to where our picnic was spread out and the women were waiting to hear the news.

We heard Father call, 'There's trouble down near Bennett's.'

'The men?' Mother asked.

'Blacks,' said Father. 'We'll go and take a look.'

'You make sure you send them on their way – they don't belong in these parts anymore,' said Mrs Walker.

Harriet and I had stepped in closer, and Mrs Walker moved aside, realising we were there.

Until that moment, I had not given a thought to the fact

that we were in our bathing costumes. They were a thin blue cotton – Mrs Walker had made us both a new set as we had so rapidly and so obviously outgrown our last ones. We had drawers that finished right above our knees and gathered at our waists. Above that, the cotton bloused out to cover our chests, buttoning up but cut low into straps that went up and over our shoulders. They were modest, but we did not have to worry ourselves about too many admiring eyes out here on the cape – and Mrs Walker had saved on fabric where she could.

I glanced across at Harriet, her wet hair snaking over her shoulders and around her neck. In this high, noon sun, I could make out all the separate droplets that beaded her skin. When I looked towards McPhail, I noticed his jaw was clenched, his eyes snagged.

When Harriet realised, it seemed as if she straightened up slightly, stood taller. As if she were meeting his gaze with her body. McPhail turned away. But I continued to watch Harriet. I thought of a red-bellied black snake I had seen one afternoon lying in the sun. It appeared to be absorbing the sun and radiating it back, making it harder and brighter and deeper.

'Girls!' said Mrs Walker, pushing two thin cotton towels at us. 'Here.'

And whatever held us there in the light – in Harriet's light – disappeared, and we took the towels and covered ourselves while the men hurried off.

As we packed up our picnic, I heard Mrs Walker mutter to Mother, 'The sooner she's in Melbourne, the better.'

'More smoke than fire,' I heard Father say as he came into the cottage that evening just before dinner. 'Some wild blacks passing through, half-a-dozen at most. Nothing to worry about, except that some of the men got their firearms out, and others told them to put them away or they'd have the Governor down here making arrests.'

'It's been a while since there's been any trouble,' Mother said.

'There's not many left. No doubt the last ones will come into the mission soon enough, hungry and sick. It's not their world anymore.'

I thought about the girl I'd seen in the vegetable patch. She did not look sick.

'As long as they're not hanging around here, I don't mind what they do,' Mother said.

'You've nothing to worry about. They're gone from here,' Father said, and the conversation moved on to talk of the dinner.

After the meal that night, Harriet and I sat on our verandah, looking out at the sky. We could see the glow from the light shining out with its beam. Blink, flash, blink.

'Will you miss this, do you think?' I asked her.

'How can I miss what is part of me? I will think of this, of all this, and of you, of course, every moment when I am there.'

'No doubt you will have many things to take up your time,' I said and laughed, but the laughter tasted sharp. It was so unfair. I was the adventurer; it was me who imagined foreign places and great cities and the hustle and bustle of a different life, and yet it was Harriet who was heading off on her own.

Harriet turned to me. 'This won't change anything,' she said, grabbing my hand. 'You know that, don't you?'

'Of course,' I said, placing my other hand on top of hers. 'Except that you will return with new dresses and a thousand new memories and a dozen suitors who would steal you off this cape and marry you in an instant.'

But Harriet was not convinced by my bravado. 'I will persuade Aunt Cecilia to invite you, too. Your mother will agree in the end – I know she will.'

'Perhaps,' I said, moving my hands away from hers. 'At any rate, I don't imagine I will be the only one who misses you.'

Harriet was quiet.

'You've noticed how he looks at you. Surely, Harriet,' I said softly.

She was silent again for a while before saying, 'I don't know what you mean.'

'Yes, you do.' I could not understand why Harriet would still not confide in me.

She looked me square in the eye. 'Truly, Kate, I don't. And I expect you don't know what you're saying either. I don't think we should speak of this again.' And she turned back to look at the darkening sky.

There it was again – the strange distance that came between us. Harriet's refusal to share her secret with me. I dreaded being left behind.

TWENTY-ONE

I told Harriet we should say goodbye to all her favourite places before she left. We were sitting side by side at the dining-room table growing despondent over the sewing Mother had set us to do, turning the hems of my brothers' pants.

Harriet peered out the small square window. 'It seems a nice enough day to go for a trek. We could go down to the cove, if you'd like.'

'Let's take the horses,' I said. 'We'll have longer at the beach that way.'

And so, as soon as we were finished, off we went.

Blaze and Sadie were pleased to be out on the track, snorting and tossing their heads. A loaf of brown bread, warm from the oven and wrapped in its calico cloth, lay tucked in the saddle bag. It was mid-morning, and the sun was everywhere: in the trees and crisscrossing the path in stripes. It seemed to tangle in Harriet's hair and illuminate the long strings of spider web across the track that were ballooning out in the breeze. A few feet ahead of us we saw the brilliant flash of a blue wren. He darted his head from side to side, jumping up and down on his twig-thin legs.

We took the horses slowly and, by the time we reached the little track that led down to the cove, it was already past lunchtime and my stomach rumbled. Up ahead, I could make out the shape of McPhail's hut through the trees.

'What about we rest at McPhail's before we go down to

the beach?' I said. 'We could sit and share our lunch if he is there?'

'Oh, let's not,' she said hastily.

'Come on, Harriet. It's hardly polite to be this close and not stop by to say hello, or goodbye, I suppose, in your case.'

I did not know what I expected of McPhail, or of Harriet. I think I desperately wanted to orchestrate a confrontation, to witness the unstoppable forces of great love, or passion, or agony, and see for myself if it was as they described in my books. Yet some part of me, the child, wanted to be reassured that I had imagined all this emotion in my mind, too filled with stories and intrigue and drama to see real life for its boring truth. Perhaps I was inventing sidelong glances, lingering hands, evidence of a lovelorn friend – to fuel the story in my head. And yet another, darker truth simmered beneath the surface; perhaps in this strange little play for three, I did not want my role but Harriet's instead.

Or perhaps I wanted to play McPhail.

Harriet looked strained, as if I had asked something terribly difficult of her. 'Briefly then,' she said. 'He won't be there anyway.'

I don't know why I expected McPhail to be home, ready to welcome us. Why would he be? He was a fisherman, and there were fish to be caught. He'd most likely been out since daybreak and would return only once he'd landed enough fish.

We reached the hut, and I tapped the door with my knuckles.

'He's not there,' Harriet said, turning to leave.

'I don't think he'd mind if we made a fire and boiled the billy.'

'Oh, Kate, we couldn't.' Harriet let out a nervous laugh.

'You don't have to come in, if you're too scared.'

'I'm not scared. Merely polite. We can't let ourselves into his home.'

'I'll call you when the tea's ready. We can have some of the bread with butter, too.'

I wiggled the handle, which turned easily in my hand, and went into the interior, dark in contrast to the brightness outside. Harriet stayed on the doorstep. The objects in the room became clearer as my eyes adjusted, and I remembered where the table sat, noted the picture on the shelf, the stove against the back wall.

I moved over to where the billy hung on its hook and tested the full weight of it. I took some kindling from the wood box and stacked it ready to take a match then ran my hand along the back of the stove to find one. My fingers picked up grease and dust until they stumbled over the square corners of the box.

I heard Harriet shuffle her feet behind me.

'Kate, this isn't right. He wouldn't like it. I don't think we should.' She spoke to me but she seemed to be trying to convince herself.

'Harriet, you worry too much. Just sit yourself down there on the step, if you can't bring yourself to come inside.'

But when I turned away from the fire, little flames now flickering bright and orange up the sticks, I saw she had entered and was standing in front of the long bench and the shelves, looking up at the picture in the frame.

I busied myself with lifting down the two tin mugs, the tin of tea, the bowl of sugar that I noticed was nearly empty, the white grains stuck hard in little clumps at the bottom.

'Who do you think she is?' Harriet nodded in the direction of the little portrait, and I moved closer to see.

The woman in the picture appeared older than us, but younger than our mothers. She was pretty enough, in a plain sort of way. The artist had painted a tie of ribbon around her neck. Her hair was dark and piled high on her head.

'I don't know,' I said, turning back to the stove. 'His mother; perhaps a fiancée. Why, what do you think?'

'I wonder what happened to her?'

'We could make up any past for her at all. For her and him. We could make it as wonderful or terrible or fanciful as we please. The stories are always better than the truth though.'

'Not always, surely,' said Harriet.

In my mind I watched the supply boat sail away towards Melbourne, Harriet waving. 'No, not always.'

Harriet leaned against the doorjamb, her figure silhouetted. She faced away from me, out to where the sea glistened through the trees.

'You won't be stuck here forever, Kate.'

The billy began to hiss, and I turned my attention to making the tea.

'Shall we sit?' I said, and pulled up a chair to the table. I cupped both hands around the mug. 'Maybe we could stay here on the cape together? We could build a hut just for us. Down on Murray's, maybe, tucked in under that old banksia?' I was grinning, and Harriet couldn't help but smile. She came over to sit with me. 'We can paint it white, like the cottages, and bring down some seedlings from the vegetable garden.'

'I could use some of Mother's old lace for curtains,' she said.

'Perfect. We can move down there and cook and clean up, then swim and lie on the beach all day.'

I met Harriet's eyes, and she looked down into her tea. Inside I felt a shift, a fracture.

'Of course, I know it's silly, Harriet,' I said, quieter now. 'It would be marvellous though, wouldn't it?'

'It would,' she said, and I had no way of knowing, as she turned to look out through the open door to the bush and then the beach beyond, if her gaze was filled with longing for the little daydream we had conjured, or for something else entirely.

'Sometimes I feel so inside out,' she said. 'As though what I'm supposed to do and what I want to do have got all mixed up and I can't even begin to untangle the two. I always thought I just wanted what I was supposed to want, but I sometimes wonder whether I might want something else.'

'What do you think you want?' I asked.

Harriet's face flushed.

'We'd better go,' she said suddenly. 'He'll be back soon. He wouldn't like to find us here.' She stood, taking up her cup.

'Maybe he would,' I said.

'Would what?'

'Would like to find us here.'

'You don't know him.' Harriet's voice was forced now, and it seemed I had tapped at some deep well of emotion.

'And you do?'

She turned on me now. 'For heaven's sake, will you leave alone this silly notion you have in your head. There is nothing between McPhail and me!'

I suddenly regretted that I had forced it. We only had a few days left together. What was I doing?

'I'm sorry, Harriet, truly,' I said, and went to her side and grabbed her hand. 'Forgive me. Please, let's not argue. Let us go to the beach as we planned and forget we ever came here.'

'Of course,' she said. 'I'm sorry, too. Let's clean up quickly.'

She walked to the door and pitched the remains of the tea onto the ground, picking up the end of her skirt to wipe around the inside of the mug. She set it gently upside down on the shelf, shifting the handle so that it was flush against the bench. She smoothed her palms down the front of her skirt, and the gesture was so like her mother's that, for a moment, I was disoriented. Harriet would make a good mother. An excellent wife.

I hurried to clean my cup, then cut two pieces of bread for us to munch on as we headed to the sand. I wondered whether, despite our careful replacing of everything we'd touched, McPhail would sense us there. He might sniff the faintest hint of Harriet's rose soap, feel the leftover warmth of the stove or be taken aback by the position of his chair, sitting closer to the table than usual so that he stumbled a little as he went to sit.

There was so sign of McPhail as we checked on the horses before following the snaking track down to the beach.

It felt disloyal but, as we walked, I wondered about

Harriet's quick anger, her reluctance to visit the hut, her questions about the woman in the picture, her certainty that he wouldn't be there. I pieced these things together, as one might lay down the squares for a patchwork quilt, and they began to make a picture. And in the picture I saw Harriet standing at the door of the hut, watched her hand go up to knock, then McPhail opening it, Harriet entering and the door closing behind her. I forced the picture from my mind.

The afternoon passed as all those afternoons had before it: we counted how many cartwheels we could make in a row before one of us fell; we collected shells; and we paddled in the shallows, splashing each other until our skirts were soaked. And we kept at it until dusk started nibbling at the corners of the sky, and we gave in to the end of the day, the last one we had at the beach before Harriet left.

TWENTY-TWO

The moment Harriet was to leave arrived all too quickly. The previous day had been filled with the hectic bluster of the supply boat arriving, the unloading of groceries, the news from town. Against all this, Harriet packed and repacked her mother's small travelling case, despite the fact that she had only her three dresses, a few petticoats and one extra pair of boots to place in there. She could not be still, and I was completely exhausted by her.

'I will look so out of place. Everyone will think me a savage!'

'You will be fine,' I soothed. 'Aunt Cecilia will have dresses made for you and you will come back and be the height of fashion around here, although there'll be hardly a soul to show.'

'Whatever will I do without you, Kate?'

'Without me?' I cried, jumping up to wrap my arms around her. 'You will have Melbourne! It is I who should be worried – it is I who will have no one.'

We kissed each other upon the cheeks at least ten times, and it was as if Harriet were leaving forever, and not just for three months, so dramatic were we.

I had promised Harriet I would watch the boat until I could see it no more. I could not bear being near the others and their excited chattering about Harriet's departure, so I announced that I'd walk to the top of the little hill off the track to the junction.

'I'll come with you,' Emmaline called, hurrying after me, perhaps thinking she might win favour by appearing to comfort me, but Mother stopped her.

'Let her be now, Em,' I heard her say.

Emmaline whined as they headed back into the kitchen to get the stocks in proper order.

It was only mid-morning, but it was hot. I kept to the shady side of the track and picked a frond of bracken to wave the flies away. I reached the spot where an opening in the bush revealed the hill path. I had to concentrate on where I trod, for the path was narrow and wound up and over tree roots and jutting rocks and I did not want to twist an ankle or fall.

It was loud with the buzzing of insects in the heat. My breath came harder as the track got steeper, and I could see the blue sky not far through the trees ahead of me now. The bush thinned out as I came closer to the top.

When I reached the rock ledge at the summit, I stopped and turned to face the way I had come. Stretched before me was the perfect half-sphere of the coastline. Looking directly below me I could follow the sandy track back to where the station was laid out. The light tower and the three cottages arranged behind it, where some of the others moved back and forth. Beyond that, the edge of the land and then the sea and the sky.

I could make out the supply boat, although from where I was I could not make out the figures on it, only its shape being tugged away by the tide and the wind.

I sat down on the rock and tried to examine the tumult inside me. In some ways I wished beyond anything that I was on that boat with Harriet. And then again, I also wished that I *was* Harriet. But there was this whispering in my head telling me that here I was, on the cape, without Harriet for the first time, really, in my whole life, and that in fact I might make something of this moment after all: something that was mine and mine alone.

'Oh,' I sighed aloud, and buried my face in my hands for it was too much to have all these confusing thoughts.

A noise startled me. Standing not ten feet from me was a black girl. I couldn't be certain, but she looked like the girl I had seen on that day in the vegetable garden with Albert, years back now. Her feet were bare, but she wore a scrappy skirt, faded to a dirty mauve, that finished halfway down her calves. She wore a man's waistcoat buttoned down, but it barely covered her. She was staring straight at me, her head tilted to one side as though she were asking me what I might be doing here instead of the other way around.

'What?' I cried and stood up. 'Go on, shoo!' I waved my hand at her to make her leave for I was a little frightened and suddenly felt a long way from the station. Who would hear me call up here, if there were others? I knew Father said they were all but gone, but she must belong with someone.

I waved my hand again. 'Go on – away with you!'

But she did not move, just flicked her eyes to where I had been watching the boat on the horizon.

'Gone,' she said, or at least that is what I thought, and I followed her gaze.

'The boat?' I said, to myself really, for I knew she could not understand a word I said.

'Gone,' she said and lifted her arm to point to where the boat was headed, then she brought her hand to the place above her left breast and said it again. 'Gone.'

I breathed out heavily in exasperation. 'Yes, the boat has gone. My friend has gone.' Futile though it was, there was some satisfaction in saying it aloud. 'She has gone to Melbourne, without me.'

The girl nodded her head and kept her hand held on the dirty cotton that scarcely covered her breast. I could not help but look there, where she held it, and I began to blush as I noticed the way her long fingers stretched across the fabric and onto the round flesh of her breast.

I had wondered at the growing fullness of my own and I

stole glances when I bathed, sometimes, coyly, cupping my hand underneath to see what it felt like. It had been a long time since Harriet and I had peered at each other's chests and giggled. I knew a blush crept up my cheeks, yet I could not look away.

She laughed and began to walk towards me, and I thought about running, all the way down the track and home, but I did not.

When she was quite close, she held out her hand and pointed to my face. Then she tapped her hand against her own cheek and spoke in her strange language. How bold she was! She repeated the sound and then came towards me, so near now, and brought up her hand to touch the sleeve of my dress. I flinched back, and she laughed and touched it again. Then she pointed to my face once more.

'Hot,' I said suddenly. 'You think I am hot.'

'Hot,' she said after me, and tapped her cheeks again and smiled.

I smiled, too, in relief. 'Kate,' I said now, and pointed at my chest. 'I'm Kate.'

She formed the word in her mouth. It did not sound quite right, but it was close enough that I felt a strange elation. She repeated the word. Then she pointed to her own chest and uttered a sound. Her name, of course, except that even when I watched her mouth closely, tried to replicate the way she stretched her lips, followed where her tongue seemed to move, I could not make anything like the sound. She said it again and again, and I tried to copy, but she just shook her head and laughed.

A loud call surprised us both, and we spun around.

A tall black man stepped from behind the scrub near the edge of the hill. He called again in his language, and the girl moved away from me and dropped her hand. I stood very still even though I thought my heart might burst through my chest. The girl stayed between me and the man, as though she might protect me. The man called again, harshly it seemed, and the girl spoke back, her chin high, and though I did not understand her, I thought it again: *she is bold*. The man spoke once more, turned, and the girl followed. She flicked her head back once and touched her hand to her cheek and I think she smiled, but maybe I imagined that, and then she disappeared over the edge, and I began to breathe again.

I told no one about the girl when I returned. In truth, I did not know what to think of my encounter. I'd not felt the righteous anger that I had when I'd seen her in our vegetable patch, the hill not being specifically part of the light station, I suppose; we were on more equal ground. As with that day, though, I still had the uneasy feeling that I was being laughed at, mocked in some way. I wondered that she was still living wild, as it were, and how many others there were. The reverend had told us when he visited last that the remaining few were being rounded up to live down on the mission at Lake Myner and that any scoundrels still at large out there in the bush would be brought in sooner or later. 'Brought in or hunted down. For their own good,' he'd said.

In the days and weeks that followed I caught myself scanning the hill for her as I went about my business, though I did not see her. I would not see her again until later, when everything had changed.

TWENTY-THREE

The days stretched and lingered while Harriet was in Melbourne. At first I came up with ways to measure the passing time: I scratched short lines in the soft rock at the base of the cliff face with a stick; I lined up shells along my windowsill; I inked the name of each day and the date in tiny letters in the back cover of a book that I knew no one else would ever open. But three months was a long time, and my rituals did not make the days pass any quicker.

Albert took the opportunity to appear before me at strange times, times when I would usually have slipped away with Harriet.

At first I resisted his invitations to clamber down the cliffs, or take the horses down the track. But the truth was, I was lonely without Harriet. I sometimes thought aloud, when my brain seized on some idea that was wonderful or silly or made me laugh, and then I would realise that Harriet wasn't there to listen, and I would bite off the end of the sentence, feeling foolish even though I was alone.

One still afternoon when the air was sticky with salt and heat, Albert approached the verandah where I was getting the cobwebs down from around the window frames with a broom. Mother had sent me out to do it, saying there was a breeze out there at least and I was better off with that chore than scrubbing the floors. But there was no breeze, and I suspected that splashing cold water over the floors would have been far more pleasant.

I pushed wet strands of hair from my forehead with a frustrated sigh and leaned on the broom as I watched him draw near.

'There's not a breath of wind. It's unbearable,' I said miserably.

'It's not a day for cleaning, I'll give you that.' He'd grown into himself these past few months and his limbs now seemed to match his height. He still didn't seem entirely comfortable in his body, but he moved more like a man and less like a boy, and I realised I found that satisfying.

'We're going down to Murray's for a swim. Your brothers and me with Harry and Ed. I wondered whether you'd like to join us?' His gaze was challenging, as if he were saying, *I know you'll say no, Kate Gilbert, but I'll damn well ask you anyway.*

It was so easy for the boys to just take off and not worry about chores, or how much help Mother needed.

'Yes,' I said. 'I'll come. My brothers won't thank you for asking me along, though. They'll say I will spoil their fun.'

Albert seemed pleased. He said he'd wait, and I put down the broom and ran inside to get my costume.

We kicked off our shoes when we arrived at Murray's, and the sand was hot beneath our feet. The sun glinted on the dimpled pelt of the water.

My brother James took off straight away. 'I'm going along to the end to search for fossils,' he told Albert, but Albert just nodded and James stomped towards the end of the beach where the rocky headland tumbled down into the sea.

'Why not stay with us?' I called after him.

'No thanks,' he yelled back, obviously annoyed that his big sister had spoiled their boys' own adventure.

Little Edward, who was as full of life at four as any child I had ever known, whooped and headed for the water, all arms and legs.

'Shouldn't you go in with him?' I asked. 'He'll be knocked over by a wave and crying to go home before we know it.'

'He can hold his own,' Albert said as he started to unbutton his shirt. 'But if it will make you feel at ease, Kate, I'll go in.'

He called to Harry and Will, who were running madly about, telling them he was going in with Edward. They thought themselves too old to play with Edward usually, but on a day as hot as this, it did not matter. On hearing Albert's call, they made straight for the water.

I stood watching them for a time. The water, the sand, the vibrant blue of the sky. Dampness spread under my arms, between my breasts, where my skin creased and stuck. Out in the shallows the boys were kicking up the water in great arcs of spray, and the droplets seemed to sparkle and glisten in the sunlight. There was nothing for it. I slipped my dress off from over my swimming costume.

I threw my hands up to the sky and spun around to feel the air cooling the sweat on my skin. I was not yet accustomed to the strange new lines of my body and where I had once felt completely at ease in the sand and the waves, running amok with Harriet or the boys, I now felt like a stranger to myself, as if I could not move so freely in the world.

When I turned back towards the sea I saw that Albert was watching me. I dropped my arms, feeling silly.

Albert raised his hand and motioned for me to join them in the water. I wiped my fingers across the coarse cotton around my waist and looked down at my pale shins, the fine dark hairs visible in the sun. Perhaps the boys would not notice that I seemed to have lost control over my shape. They just wanted to play. I ran down the sand to join them.

The first brush of the water against my toes was deliciously cold, and I squealed and ran back from the edge.

Harry squawked in delight. 'She's in, she's in!' he cried, and bent low to scoop his hands through the water and splash me.

I arched away as the spray hit me, a hundred pinpoints of cold against my bare arms, my neck.

I splashed back, and then it was all kicking and laughing

and great sprays of glittering water, the sharp cold and the hot sun, the briny seaweed scent of the day. Whatever charge I had thought there had been between Albert and me unspooled and rolled out in the sun and the wind, and we were like children again, splashing and squealing and running away only to come back with greater force to splash and splash again.

When we eventually tired, we left the water and flung ourselves down on the hard wet sand that the receding tide had left behind. We lay like starfish, toes aimed up to the sky, the three younger boys in between Albert and me, our arms shielding our eyes from the sun.

I turned my chin to press my lips against the skin of my shoulder and felt its coolness, the tang of salt when I pulled my lips away. I thought of the water babies, and young Tom, cleaned of all his soot and grime and unhappiness as he discovers the new world, washed clean by the river.

I remembered some lines from the book, and I spoke them aloud to my audience of four.

Strong and free, strong and free,
The floodgates are open, away to the sea.
Free and strong, free and strong,
Cleansing my streams as I hurry along,
To the gold sands, and the leaping bar,
And the taintless tide that awaits me afar,
As I lose myself in the infinite main,
Like a soul that has sinned and is pardoned again.

It felt like a song on my tongue, and the words lingered on in the space around us even after I was silent.

'Again, again,' cried little Edward, and I reached over to run my hand through his damp hair.

'I don't understand it. What is it?' said Harry.

'Sounds like a load of nonsense to me,' said Albert, and he stood, brushing the sand off his woollen trunks as his eyes met mine.

I frowned.

'I mean, it's lovely, how you say it. You make it sound lovely.' He looked contrite now, but the damage was done.

I sat up. 'It's from *The Water Babies*, Harry, and I wouldn't expect your ignorant brother to understand. I never saw him pick up a book, even in the schoolhouse.'

Albert dropped his head and stormed off along the beach. Edward's face fell as he watched his big brother, but he was soon distracted by Will and Harry, who found a sponge that resembled a ball and a stick that could do as a bat. They marked out a pitch, and we all had goes bowling the dried sponge at each other. We laughed, and they seemed not to mind at all having a girl in their midst, especially one who could bowl as hard as I could.

Every now and then, though, I looked down the beach after Albert. I hadn't meant to hurt his feelings, but he had scorned my poetry.

'Good ball, Harry!' I called as Ed swung wildly with the bulbous end of the banksia branch and Will raced to grab the sponge where it had landed. I clapped my hands together.

I could see Albert kicking his long white legs at small black objects on the sand, which spun up into the air in a spray of sand. James was still nowhere to be seen, off in the rocks somewhere, searching for his fossils. *Serves them both right to be alone*, I thought. *Spoilsports*.

The younger boys started to tire, and I pulled my dress on over my costume, now dry and stiff with salt. I hoped that Albert and James would see I was gathering our things and brushing off the boys, helping them into their shirts and trousers.

The sun was dipping low in the sky now, and out across the sheltered nook of the bay, the entire surface of the water rippled with gold light. Just when I thought I would have to call out for them, soften my voice with kindness and apology, Albert came back up the beach with James trailing behind. We gathered up the rest of our things and made our way off the beach, into the lengthening shadows of the track back towards the station.

The bird calls were raucous, echoing in and out and about the canopy and the underbrush. The last rays of the afternoon filtered through the leaves as though through green lace, and it seemed that there was so much to see and hear and smell that it did not matter that Albert and I did not speak.

When we were in sight of the lighthouse the other boys dashed ahead, Harry calling to his father, who held a mallet raised to strike at a fence post.

'Your father works hard,' I said, because it was true and my annoyance at Albert had faded with the afternoon. I thought we should be on speaking terms when we returned.

Albert was a little ahead of me, and he stopped and turned around so abruptly that I almost ran into him.

'Yes, you're smarter than me, Kate Gilbert. Everyone knows it. But it doesn't mean that I'm not good enough for you.'

I could not speak. I was astonished.

'My father says,' he went on, a little breathless and red now, 'he says there's nothing to stop me asking for your hand, and your parents would be lucky to have such a fine and hard-working lad as me as their son-in-law, and even though Mother thinks you are hot-headed and not as pretty as you are quick, my father says it doesn't mean you won't make a good wife.'

I opened my mouth and closed it again, once, twice, perhaps even three times, before I could force any sound out. And then it came all in one breath, hot and sour.

'Then your father is mistaken. For I will not make a good wife and I will certainly never be yours.'

I pushed past him, blinking fast and shaking, and when I was a little distance from him and heard him calling my name, I ran.

TWENTY-FOUR

Mrs Walker had convinced her husband that it was necessary he make the two-day trek to Edenstown to pick up a tonic for her nerves, and that she couldn't wait until the supply boat next month. We all knew that the only tonic she needed was a letter from Harriet, and that Walker would also return with that. In fact Harriet had also included a letter for me, and I took it breathlessly from Mrs Walker when she arrived at the cottage door, showing no sign of her previous nervous condition at all.

I rushed to hide the letter beneath my pillow so that I might savour the anticipation of reading it. I was missing her desperately, especially when everything seemed so topsy-turvy in her absence.

It wasn't until after dinner that night – once the washing up, the wiping down, the setting out of the dough for the morning, the heating up of water for a bath, the corralling of the children, the prayers and the goodnights were done – that I could take out Harriet's letter.

'What's that?' said Emmaline, her little eyes peering like marbles in the semi-dark from her side of the room.

'Nothing.'

'Yes, it is. It's a letter.'

'If you knew already, then why did you ask?' I turned away from her so that she could not see.

'You don't have to be so short with me,' she said in a manner designed to make me feel wretched.

'It's only that it's a letter from Harriet and I haven't even had a moment to open it yet, and I'm desperate for news.'

'I suppose you must be, for she is your best friend,' she said in that quiet, wounded voice again.

I slid my thumbnail along the top edge of the envelope.

'I wish there was a girl my age on the cape,' Emmaline said sullenly.

'Emmaline, I promise I will tell you all about it in the morning if you will only hush now and go to sleep so I might read it myself.'

There was a dramatic huffing and loud shuffling of covers and, when it ceased, I finally unfolded the letter and consumed it in one go.

Oh, to hear her voice, there in ink on the page! It was as though she were chattering in my ear. I brought the pages to my face to sniff out any trace of my friend but all I encountered was the acrid smell of the ink.

After I had read the letter three times, I folded it and slid it between the pages of the book on my nightstand. Turning the lantern down slowly until it spluttered out, I stared up at the dense darkness around me.

So Harriet had an admirer. It was to be expected, of course. Her mother had probably always anticipated that Harriet would come home with a proposal and that she herself would then accompany her daughter off the cape and make arrangements for an engagement, a wedding, a new future.

I was truly happy for my friend. I pulled my bedclothes up to my neck and closed my eyes, but I knew I would not sleep. I took my happiness for Harriet in regard to her admirer, this Patrick, and examined it as one would a jewel. I held it out from myself and looked for signs of cracks and fissures in the emotion, places where it was shadowed, but it seemed to be pure. Intact. I did wonder if some of the glitter of this feeling came from the fact that it was a *new* admirer who had caught Harriet's eye, and that it might mean she would not bother with the eyes that looked upon her when she was home at the station.

Because here on the cape, things were complicated enough. Albert and I were not speaking. His half-formed proposal sat like a big solid rock between us. At times, I was livid that he had spoken to me in such a way; and at others, I felt my chest expanding with pleasure: pleasure in his asking but the greatest pleasure in my refusal. I remembered the way it had felt when I saw how crushed he was by my response and how I had savoured the power in that. It made me grander and diminished me in equal parts, and I was having trouble working out what it meant.

I would not mention any of this to Harriet when I replied to her. I knew that she would shriek and clap her hands over her mouth at the thought of a proposal, any proposal, but it was her face, when she took in that it was Albert Jackson who had proposed, that I could not bear imagining. He was just a boy, in her mind. Not a dashing young heir from Melbourne. Not a brooding, salt-eyed fisherman. A boy from the lighthouse, more like a brother really.

In truth, it was not Albert himself who was the problem. What angered me was the thought that he had assumed to speak to his father of a possible marriage to me, as though I were an item that could be bargained over. Perhaps all marriage proposals were in some way business transactions – but this I could not abide. If this were the case then surely I would never marry. The thought of standing by Albert's side, while our parents celebrated and nodded their heads knowingly. *See*, they would say, *she was the marrying type after all*. Oh, it made my skin crawl to think of it.

But there was something Albert could offer. It flickered in me and flipped my heart about. He wanted me. If he had mulled over the idea of marriage, then surely he had imagined what it might entail. Had he lain in his narrow bed at night, looking up into the darkness and thinking about me? Had he imagined a different ending to his muttered proposal, one where I looked down, bit my lip, placed my hand on his arm? One where he stepped forwards, bold beyond his true self, and lifted my chin so I must meet his eyes. Where slowly, ever so slowly, while the twilight ceased to exist around us, he pulled me closer to him and leaned his face down towards mine. I shut my eyes. Then his lips were upon mine, dry and cool, and it was as though he were touching me everywhere and not just that one spot, as though his touch had broken open the sky. And then all of my body was against him, wanting his chest to open up so that I could climb inside, all of him meeting all of me. I moved my hands up to grasp his face and pull him in ever closer, but my hands encountered the thick scratchiness of a beard, and when I opened my eyes, in this dream, in Albert's dream, I was kissing McPhail and he was kissing me. And we did not stop.

In the bed next to mine Emmaline stirred, and I rolled over, away from her. Clenching my eyes tight, I tried to hold on to the picture, even as it broke up like high summer cloud and drifted away.

TWENTY-FIVE

I escaped the next afternoon and wandered down to the point. It was not the same without Harriet. I could have asked Emmaline to come with me but, in truth, I was feeling flustered from my dreams and needed to be on my own.

I took a roundabout way and found I didn't have the energy to cross the gorge when I got to it, so instead I nestled into a ledge next to a large clear pool. I let my fingers trail across the surface of the water, swirling and twirling the reflection so it appeared that I was curdling the clouds above with the tips of my fingers.

Out to sea there was a shearwater, white and black and grey, moving in great slow circles above the waves. Around and around it went, drawing me into its eddy. Suddenly the bird folded in on itself, pointing its long neck towards the water to form an arrow. Down it plunged, a black streak across the sky, entering the water with a tiny flurry of white foam.

I scanned the surface of the water, but the bird did not reappear. And then, there it was, a glint of silver flapping in its beak. Slowly, wings beating furiously, it pulled itself away from the surface of the sea. Up and up and up it went, higher and higher until I could not make it out in the sky anymore.

'Where are you going with that then?' I mused out loud.

'With what?' There was a deep voice behind me, and I shot up as though I had been stung by a bull ant. I turned sharply and found myself looking at McPhail, his fishing rod held loosely in one hand and an amused expression on his face.

'You scared me!' I cried, scowling at him. 'What were you thinking, frightening me like that?'

'I didn't see you there,' he said, and went to walk past me.

I was sure he could see the red creeping slowly up my neck. I could not look him in the eye for fear that he would read my mind and know that I had spent last night dreaming of kissing him.

'Well, don't do it again.' And even as I said it I blushed further at how ridiculous I sounded.

'Wouldn't dream of it,' he said over his shoulder as he walked out to where the waves were splashing up onto the rocks.

I chastised myself for my childish response. Damn McPhail. Damn my stupid dreams. Damn Harriet for not being here so we could laugh about it and I could throw his smugness right back at him.

I looked over to where he was crouched next to his satchel, rummaging about. That was just the thing, though, wasn't it? Harriet had always been there, making me braver and louder and tougher. Being the beautiful one, the kind one, the one who was altogether more genteel.

I picked my way over the rocks towards him, determined to prove that I wasn't a child.

'What do you suppose you'll catch, then?' I called when I was quite close. If I startled him he didn't show it.

'Mullet. Rockling perhaps.'

'Not out in the boat today?'

'Went early. Caught the tide.'

He was a man of few words.

But I wanted to keep talking to him. 'I've not seen you fish here before.'

'Thought I'd find a new hole.'

I moved to his side and sat down on a rock next to a small pool.

'Didn't realise it was your spot,' he added.

I laughed, too primly, and swallowed it back. 'Of course it's not my spot. I was just out walking, and found a place to rest.'

I bent over the pool and broke the surface of the water with my hand, stretching my fingers down so they appeared to wobble and wave like the strands of plump green pearls in the Neptune's necklace.

I tried to think of something to say. To show that while I might not be beautiful, I was clever and thoughtful and quick. I remembered the notes I'd seen on one of Father's maps, notes that made my eyes wide with curiosity when I read them.

'They used to say there was an inland sea,' I began, 'that stretched straight across the middle of this country.'

McPhail made a *humph* sound in the back of his throat – part amused, part dismissive. 'There's no inland sea.' He cast the line so that the sinker splashed a good few yards out and disappeared into the waves.

'How can you be so sure?' I questioned, turning towards him. 'You haven't travelled across the country in its entirety, have you?'

McPhail didn't look at me, but he replied easily. 'No. No, I haven't.'

'Then how can you know?' I said, smiling but trying to sound cross. I was artless in the manner of conversing with men, I realise this now. There was none of Harriet's coy knowing in me; it was all childlike inquisitiveness or else a blushing awareness of how utterly lacking in guile I was.

He ran his forefinger down the length of line where his hand rested. It was an odd movement – gentle and restrained – for a man of his size. His eyes did not move from the ocean.

'There's nothing in the centre,' he said. Softly, as though he were speaking of something he oughtn't. 'Just sand and heat. Freezing cold nights and the calls of strange dogs and those wild blacks singing their songs. There's no sea in there.' He pulled the rod in against his chest, testing the tension.

I was not used to being told I was wrong with such authority. 'It doesn't sound very nice at all.'

'No,' he said in that same quiet voice. 'No, nice isn't a word you could use.'

'I suppose that's why you like the coast so much, then.'

'Something like that.'

'Well, there isn't much else here one can like, is there?'

I was trying to get his attention, make him realise that I was more than just a girl. I was very nearly a woman; I was just the same as Harriet. Why on earth did he not look at me the way he'd looked at her? How could he so calmly hold his line there and not even glance my way?

He reeled back suddenly, the rod bowing so that it arced and quivered, and he turned the line over and over in his hands. When I peered into the waves where his line threaded in, I could see a silvery flash. Then he was plucking it out, bending the rod and pulling the line so that the fish fairly popped out of the water. It landed on the edge of the rock. McPhail leaned down and pinned it with his hand.

I stepped forwards to get a closer look, and suddenly he thrust the rod at me. I took hold and he lifted up the fish with both hands. Slipping his forefinger and thumb in under the gills, he tugged sharply and a splash of blood spurted across his hand. McPhail turned to me, holding the fish by the throat and letting it hang so I could see its size and weight.

I could not have said that he was smiling, but there was a glint in his eye, and his face had a liveliness it had not had before.

'Ah, but there's enough to like,' he said.

TWENTY-SIX

In the days that followed it was as though I were in a fever of sorts. And through it all I felt as though every person with whom I came in contact must know the contents of my thoughts and dreams. Surely my mother, as we kneaded the dough for our bread and placed it in tins, must realise that my thoughts were not on the spongy dough but on the silhouette of McPhail against the sea and sky, on those words that ricocheted around my mind: *there's enough to like*. What could he mean? Surely he was referring to Harriet. But could he mean me?

'Careful, Kate,' warned my mother, as I lingered too long at the mouth of the oven with the loaf tin. 'Where's your head today?'

Everywhere, Mother, and nowhere but with him. That is what I wanted to say.

'I miss Harriet,' is what I said instead. And I did. Of course.

Mother wiped her hands on her apron. 'Won't be long now till she's home again. I dare say it's done you both some good to get out of each other's pockets for a few months.'

I brushed the flour from the benchtop into my cupped hand. 'Yes, I suppose it has.'

Harriet would be home soon, a week at most before the supply boat was due to bring her. And wouldn't it be wonderful to have her back, to watch her eyes shine wide with the news she would tell me, to walk our favourite tracks again, to lie on our backs in the sun and be lazy with the warmth of each other.

And yet. There would be no more moments with McPhail. Harriet would pull him back into her orbit, and I would be invisible again. I picked dough from my fingers.

'Do you need me this afternoon, Mother?'

'No more than usual.'

'It's just, I thought I might take one of the horses for a ride along the track. Get some air.' Such a small thought at first, half formed at most.

Mother took three onions from the barrel and set them on the board. 'Take Sadie, then. You can meet the children as they come back from the schoolhouse,' she said.

That would not work for my plan at all. 'I hadn't intended to go that way. Sadie doesn't like the loose rock on the path.'

'Oh, she'll be alright. Just take her slow.'

Perhaps I could make it down to the hut and then cut back inland to get to the schoolhouse road in time. But not on Sadie. I'd have to take Shadow. It was a risk, I knew; he was sure to be frisky, but he would go fast. But what was I thinking? The hut would be empty. It was ridiculous.

I untied my apron. 'I suppose I could meet the children.'

'Careful that you take it slow,' Mother repeated.

I grabbed my hat as I went through the front door and forced myself to keep a steady gait until I got round to the side of the house. Then I ran.

Shadow was wary as I approached and quickly heaved the saddle onto him.

'Shush, boy,' I said, down low in his ear at the same time as I dug my heels in to show him who was in charge.

He threw his head around and resisted my direction, but I held fast.

There was hardly time to reach the hut, let alone be back to meet the children on the track. And if I didn't get back, how would I explain where I had been? I kicked my heels again and spurred him on.

I was down there in about half an hour, as quick as I'd ever done it, and as I rode through the trees I saw McPhail. My chest clenched. He was working at the wood pile beside the hut. He lifted his head at the sound of the horse.

In my hurry to get there I hadn't given a thought to what I would say to the man. *Enough to like*, he'd said. He'd said it and Harriet wasn't here, hadn't been here for almost three months. All I had to do, surely, was to give him the opportunity to expand on his phrase.

I pulled Shadow up and jumped down. 'Hello there!' I called.

'Afternoon,' he called back. 'What brings you down here?'

Think, Kate. Think.

'I'm off to collect the children from school. Thought I'd come for a bit of a ride on my way.'

Oh, Kate, how stupid, how unconvincing.

'Right,' he said, and went back to his pile of wood.

'And how are you?' I said as I approached him.

'No different from usual.'

'Lovely that it's cooling down some, isn't it?'

''Tis.'

Each time he raised the axe, his lips parted at the effort of plunging the blade into the wood. He had left his usual waistcoat off for the work, and his shirtsleeves were rolled up so that I could see the muscles tensing in his forearms.

'Albert's proposed to me,' I blurted out.

There was not even a pause before he replied, 'You'd do well to accept him.'

'I will not.'

'No doubt he will be disappointed.'

I took a few steps closer to where he stood. I was conscious that some of my hair had come loose on the ride. I flicked it so that it lay behind one shoulder, so that my neck was bare.

'Oh, I suppose he will. He'll get over it,' I said.

McPhail raised the axe and let it swing. It cut, deep and true, into the heart of the log.

I waited for him to say something more, to disagree, to flatter me. But he did not. Disappointment curdled my stomach, and something else: the fury that he would not notice me. *Look at me*, I wanted to shout. *Why will you not look at me and see me, too? Can I be that unattractive that I cannot ignite some desire in you?* I would be bold. An image of the black girl appeared in my mind.

'You are strong to cut the wood so,' I said, and moved closer to McPhail. 'Albert is still a boy.'

He stopped chopping, but only long enough to catch his breath and throw another log to the side. He made no comment and lifted the axe again.

I find it difficult to recall what I did next because of the terrible, hot shame of it.

I went closer, the thrill of the axe whistling through the air making the little hairs on the nape of my neck tingle and stand on end.

He stopped again but did not look at me.

'Better stand back. The wood can splinter. Don't want you hurt.'

If only he hadn't said the last part; the way he said *you*. It made me bolder.

'I don't want to stand back,' I said.

He looked at me finally and must have seen through me so completely, all of my desire and neediness on show. But he did nothing, so I moved towards him and reached out my hand to place it on his arm and, when I touched him, he flinched and arched back away from me and dropped the axe.

'You'd best go home,' he almost shouted as he turned and strode inside his hut.

At first I froze, so humiliated that I thought I might vomit. Then I ran towards Shadow and fumbled and fumbled with his saddle before I was up and pulling tight on the reins. Shadow snorted with delight as I forced him to race back up the track we had so recently flown down with the same kind of fever.

I was like a storm when I got back to the house.

'Where are the children?' Mother called, and to my horror I realised I had forgotten that I had been going to meet them.

'I could not wait!' I yelled back as I ran to my room and slammed the door. I was appalled by what I had done. By how McPhail had rebuffed me. By what I had imagined might happen between us.

'Oh!' I cried in fury and threw myself onto my bed as hot tears spilled down my cheeks.

My face was soon a mess of snot and tears. I sat up to get a handkerchief from the dresser beside my bed, pulling on the top drawer, but it was jammed. The harder I pulled the more stuck it became until I yelled in a rage, 'Damn it! Damn it!'

I had never felt more at odds with myself, so incapable of stopping the way I was acting.

I must have appeared quite mad when Mother burst in with Emmaline, freshly back from school, and exclaimed, 'Good grief, Kate! Whatever are you doing?'

I could not explain my rage or the upturned drawer or my sudden tears except to say that I was hot and not myself and missing Harriet dreadfully.

TWENTY-SEVEN

And then Harriet was back. We were all waving from the jetty as the boat arrived, and she was standing at the prow, with a new hairstyle, taller and more curved, or so it seemed. It was all I could do to hold myself back so that her mother could embrace her first. Then we were upon each other, hugging and kissing and crying with delight.

'How I've missed you!' I said, and could not fathom the relief and the fizzle inside me that bubbled up and over to be held by Harriet again.

The last of the heat seemed to vanish after Harriet returned, and autumn was upon us. We were to have a bonfire, burning an old fence that had just been knocked down and was riddled with ants. The grey planks were thrown together, along with armfuls of dead underbrush that had been cleared to form a new track. By the time the pile towered over us, we were jumpy with excitement.

Father was especially jovial at dinner and wanted to get the fire going before he had to go up and light the lamp. He hurried Mother along, and she scolded him as he playfully tugged her apron. She did not really mind at all. Their happiness infused the kitchen, and I felt a warm glow deep inside because life seemed good again – the relaxed joy of my parents, the anticipation of the fire, Harriet's return. I should have known it could not last.

The bonfire was set down from the cottages in the outer

paddock where we usually kept the goats. Mother and Mrs Walker had ushered them into the house paddock so that they wouldn't be frightened by the fire. We made our way past them, our arms filled with blankets, and also with bags of potatoes to throw onto the coals.

As I laid out the blankets, back a way from the great pile, I noticed Albert, helping his father to add yet more sticks, odds and ends, and refuse from the cottages to the pyre. We had hardly spoken since that day coming home from the beach, weeks before. He had avoided me, and I him.

I had not uttered a word of what occurred between Albert and me to Harriet, and I would never reveal what I had done when I went to McPhail's hut. So much had happened in her absence and yet she knew nothing of it. She was back, and I was content to bask in the stories of her time in the city.

I ignored Albert now and hoped desperately that McPhail would not take up Mother's invitation to the bonfire.

I spotted Harriet coming down the slope from her cottage and called out to Father that it was surely time that Harriet and I lit the bonfire, for it was getting late.

'And why should you and Harriet be the ones to light the fire?' my father said, his eyes sparkling with good humour.

'To celebrate Harriet's homecoming,' I called back, made bold by my father's mood.

Jackson raised his glass, which appeared to be empty already. 'Seems only fair that the girls get their own little party.'

Harriet and I clasped hands and ran to where the men stood. I saw Albert glance over at us, a strange expression crossing his face, as though he had stubbed his toe and was trying to hold in the pain of it for fear of the mocking he might receive.

Father handed Harriet the matches and me a small tin of kerosene.

'Careful now, Kate,' he said. 'Away from your skirts, right into the centre of the thing, to set her off.'

144

Mother had moved closer and looked concerned as she watched me with the tin. I saw that, behind her, McPhail had indeed arrived. Harriet had not noticed yet, concentrating as she was on the matchbox in her hand. Mother passed McPhail a bottle of ale, and he took a long draught of it before he looked our way. I lowered my eyes quickly.

'C'mon then, Kate, throw it in!' Jackson spoke more boisterously than usual, and I marvelled at the strange effect ale could have on a man, and how stupid it could make him appear.

I pitched the small round mouth of the drum away from me and a clear stream of fluid arced up and into the nest of wood.

Harriet was having trouble lighting the match, but finally it sparked and she flung the lit match into the pile.

It was a good throw. For a second it seemed as though it would not catch. There was no sign of flames, and we all leaned forwards, and then smoke appeared through the branches. A popping sound followed. Flames appeared and climbed higher.

We all stepped back as one from the heat. The bonfire glowed, and orange embers danced in the updraught of heat.

Albert was opposite, staring at me, his face gentle and hurt and happy at the same time. The fire was roaring now, and the thrill was extraordinary, and I could not help but smile at him.

Suddenly, he was beside me.

'Isn't it wonderful?' he said, looking at the flames.

'It is.' I was aware of Harriet's presence on my other side. A thread of tension vibrated through me.

The fire crackled and hissed, and a long branch lost its place and fell towards where we stood, landing with a flurry of red sparks. Harriet and I drew back instinctively, and Albert stepped forwards, bending low and grabbing the stick where it had not burned and flinging it back into the fire.

'Are you alright?' he asked, his face showing his concern.

I felt Harriet's eyes searching mine, her interest piqued by the warm tone Albert had used.

'Of course,' I said, and stepped a little closer to Harriet, a little further away from Albert. I was being deliberately unkind now, but it seemed my earlier smile had encouraged him.

'I wonder if the ships at sea will see the fire, when it gets dark,' he said.

It was the type of question I might have asked, and I considered whether he had conceived it on purpose, in an effort to remind me we were similar.

'Perhaps,' I replied and put my arm out to touch Harriet's shoulder. 'Look there,' I said to her, 'what the children are doing.'

Will and Harry were milling conspiratorially on the opposite side of the fire from us. As we watched, Harry stepped forwards and threw something small straight into the heart of the fire. The flame there flared, and the sound of a crack, like a whip lashing, resounded in the air around us.

Mrs Walker gasped, and the boys erupted into fits of giggles.

Harriet and I laughed, and I noticed that Harriet covered her mouth with her hand as she did so, a gesture I'd never seen her do before. Perhaps ladies in Melbourne were not encouraged to laugh out loud. *How dreadful*, I thought, but I, too, raised my hand to my face in a mirror of Harriet's, just to see what it felt like.

'Harold!' called Albert, and his face grew stormy as he charged around to the other side of the bonfire and proceeded to give his brother and mine a stern talking to.

The fire had emboldened the boys, and instead of cowering under the spray of words they were receiving from Albert, they laughed openly. Harry, taunting him, threw again. Another whip crack and more gasping, and I saw Albert clench his fists by his sides.

It was not right for the boys to treat him so. I, too, knew the frustrations of trying to get the younger children to take heed of my instructions. The infuriation when my words were ignored, the hot indignation of a younger child talking back as if I knew nothing.

Beside me, Harriet spoke. 'Emmaline mentioned you and Albert have been friendly these past months while I was away. I'm glad you had someone to talk to when I wasn't here.'

She was looking over at Albert, who had taken Harry roughly by the shoulder and was marching him away from the fire. Her words had the hint of another meaning.

'No more than usual,' I said. It would have been a great relief to tell Harriet all that had happened, but I sensed that I was at a disadvantage. That Melbourne had taken my Harriet and whirled her around and she had come back to me somehow altered from before. She seemed separate from all of us on the cape now; better, in fact.

'Have you fought?' Harriet asked. 'Emmaline said there was some disquiet between you. What did you fight about?'

What did Emmaline know of it? Had she been spying on me? Had Albert divulged details to her? The thought of it! Or maybe I was not as secretive with my feelings as I hoped. I tried to keep my face from giving anything away. She knew me, Harriet. She read me like a fisherman reads the tides. If I wasn't careful she would have the whole story out of me just from my expression, a few evasive words.

'I don't know what Emmaline thinks she knows – everything is as it has always been.'

Albert continued to hold his brother roughly; they had stopped near the edge of the paddock, and I saw Harry's chin jut up, and the sudden movement of Albert swiping his hand out to cuff Harry on the ear.

Harriet nodded in their direction. 'Perhaps he is practising for fatherhood and is trying to keep the younger ones in line.'

She smirked, and I blushed, fiercely, the skin prickling along my jaw.

'The young men I met in Melbourne, they did not act so coarsely. It is a shame, out here, that boys like Albert will not get a chance to better themselves, to move off the cape. As I have done. As you will.'

Was Harriet so far apart from me now? Why was she

making the distance so plain? I was hurt by her assessment of Albert who, despite our feud, was my friend and had been for some time. And while he had spoken out of turn and was oftentimes shy and clumsy, he was a fine brother and son, and had recognised my loneliness while Harriet was away and had been kind in his wish to relieve me of it.

I took the opportunity to steer our conversation to this new topic. 'Do you really think I will?'

'What?' she asked.

'Move away from here?'

Harriet laughed, and this time did not hide her mouth. 'Of course you will, Kate. There is nothing for us here. You will visit Melbourne as I did, and you will be introduced to fine young men as I was, and then there will be a letter and a proposal and you will be whisked off this damned cape and be married and have a grand house and children, and a husband who will not have to tend to a light, but will tend to you.' She gazed into the fire as she spoke.

I had never wanted that. Adventure, yes; travel, too. But I had always imagined myself returning. Following the tides that would lead me back home when it was time. I had not imagined life in another home, one where I would be the mistress.

Albert had finished with Harry and was hurrying back around the fire to us. I saw Father conferring with the other men and setting off for the lighthouse. McPhail, too, was taking his leave, and I noticed that he hardly looked back at us girls. It was for the best, I thought. I could not possibly hold myself together if he were to approach Harriet and me; I would surely die of mortification.

'The troublemakers, throwing old shot,' Albert said when he arrived back to stand next to me. 'I taught them a lesson.'

His self-satisfaction made me wince, for I knew that Harriet, in her high and mighty mood from Melbourne, would not be kind.

'You did, did you?' she said. She pointed to where the boys

148

had resumed their mischief. 'They obviously take you very seriously.'

I looked down at my boots. Albert was not used to this meanness from Harriet, and neither was I. It was at once unflattering and exciting.

'Well, they are boys, I s'pose. What should we expect?' He laughed awkwardly and appealed to me for agreement.

But Harriet had shifted something in me. With Harriet's eyes, I saw Albert again as little more than a child and nothing like a man.

'You are wrong to hit your brother like that, Albert. He is only young and' – I paused for effect – 'you are not much older than him yourself.'

Harriet nodded at me in approval.

Albert dug the toe of his boot into the dry soil. 'I suppose you and Harriet have much to catch up on now that she has returned.' He said it so softly I could barely hear him.

When he looked up at me I detected a trace of scorn in his blue eyes. As though I were not the girl he thought I was and yet was everything he predicted.

I could not ignore the hollowness I felt as he walked away, and Harriet grabbed my arm and pulled me in close and said, 'Isn't it best when it's just the two of us?'

TWENTY-EIGHT

I'd convinced Harriet to go down to Blackman's Bay to collect mussels for the afternoon. It was a sheltered little spot, not far from Bennett's River, and the fishermen often kept their boats there when the wind was blowing rough.

It had been two days and, until now, we'd not had a chance to escape on our own. Mrs Walker's hovering, and then blustery winds and abrupt rain showers, had kept us indoors and apart, but this day had cracked open with brilliant sunshine, the kind that reflected the recent rain in the air and glittered amongst the leaves.

We took the horses, me out in front on Blaze and Harriet behind on Sadie, who ambled slowly and I had to keep pulling on my reins and holding Blaze back so that I could ask Harriet about Melbourne. I batted questions at her, and she responded with vivid descriptions of imposing buildings and parties and shopping in grand stores. Aunt Cecilia had shown Harriet off as something of a rarity, exotic in her remoteness, unspoiled by the dirt and flurry and downtrodden aspects of Melbourne.

She had called a barber and had Harriet's hair styled in the latest fashion. A man with an oiled moustache had lopped at least six inches off the bottom of her curls. Harriet shuddered as she told me he'd singed the cut ends with a match and the room had filled with the acrid tang of her burned hair.

'It took everything I had not to burst into tears right there in front of him and Aunt Cecilia. To burn my hair! It was criminal. I could smell the awful stink of it for days. I waited till I could shut myself in my room, complaining of a headache, and I had a good cry into my pillow. How I missed you and Mother and all at the cape that day.'

While Harriet spoke, we rounded the last hill, and the bay and the little jetty were laid out below us.

'Oh, Kate, see – this is what I missed.'

I had to admit it looked particularly lovely that day. It was as if the sun had been spilled onto the surface of the sea and was broken only by small white caps whipped up by the breeze. Even so, I was still caught up in the tale of the barber: imagining my hair being cut off so that I didn't have to bother with it anymore, then stepping out into the Melbourne bustle with a new style, a new me, in a place I could get lost or be found.

'It's always here, though, isn't it, Harriet? Even after you've been away – it's here, the same.'

'I suppose. But the world out there is not always as wonderful as I expected it to be.'

'Well, there were certainly more beaus to turn your head! Tell me again about Patrick.'

'It was nothing at all, really.'

'That's not what the contents of your letter suggested.' I laughed. 'Oh, you should have heard your mother after she got your letter and she came to tell mine all about it. "Harriet's caught the eye of a proper young gentleman!" she said, and Mother put the kettle on and they both sat down and swatted me away as they pored over your letter and I tried to work out if there was anything you had written to your mother that you had failed to tell me. That you had been to a party. That you had worn a green dress. That this young man was the son of a wealthy landowner with a great swathe of sheep. That he had spoken to you and ignored the other young ladies. That he had asked if he might call on you again. That you had taken a turn around the gardens, with your aunt chaperoning, of course. That you appeared spoken for.'

'Goodness, Kate, you know everything there is to know of the story already. That's all there was, honestly.'

I couldn't see her face and wondered if she were telling the truth.

'But you saw him again?'

'Only once more after that. He insisted he would write, though.'

'What did he look like? Was he very handsome?'

'He was.' Harriet paused. 'It was as if he had stepped out of a painting of the city. I mean, he looked exactly as he should look. He wore a top hat and a fine suit, out of an excellent wool – or so my aunt told me – and he had the blondest hair.'

I had to stop Blaze there, for the track grew too narrow, and we both climbed down, tied the horses up and made our slow way down to the jetty.

The bristled leaves of the saltbush and prickly Moses caught at our skirts, and we were red in the face and breathless by the time we reached the steps hewn straight out of the cliff. They led us down towards the little rocky bay and the greying timber of the jetty, jutting out into the sea.

It was hard to continue our conversation during the descent, our voices snatched away by the wind, but when I turned to Harriet to take her hand and help her down the first steep step, I asked her one last question about her beau.

'What did you speak of? What did he say to you?'

At this Harriet blushed. She gazed out to sea, and there was a long moment before she replied.

'I felt I knew nothing. That I had nothing worth speaking of. Melbourne is so full of people and buildings and life, just bursting with it all, Kate, truly, I cannot describe it to you. I felt as though everything I had to say came from this little cape, that I knew nothing of the world. I felt like a child.'

'You're seventeen now, Harriet. You're hardly a child. And I bet you could have taught Patrick a thing or two about hard work and lighthouses and the tides and the sea.' I was indignant for my friend, for us both. For if she could feel as though her whole life amounted to nothing in the face of the sophistication of the city, how would I feel if I ever had the chance to go?

I jumped down onto the next step and took Harriet's hand again as she followed me.

'Oh, he was nice about it all. He talked to me about growing up on the land. And I suppose he thought it was rather exciting that I lived in a lighthouse. No one in the city could understand that I didn't live in the actual tower so in the end I stopped trying to explain the cottages and the settlement as people only seemed bored.'

'See them be bored by this!' I said, and spread my arms out before us.

Harriet looked out and smiled. She stepped down again, reaching for my hand and, as she did, her foot slipped, a loose rock shooting ahead of her and glancing off me as it sailed down the rock steps.

I put my arms out to break Harriet's fall, but she landed heavily, stumbling awkwardly on one leg, a little yelp of pain issuing from her lips.

'Harriet! Here, sit down, lean on me.' I helped her to sit, and she winced as she stretched out her left leg.

'I've twisted my ankle.'

'It'll be alright. Let me take a look.'

Harriet muttered to herself as I loosened the laces on her boot. I could feel the heat through her stockings where the flesh was already swelling.

I turned and looked down at the dozen steps, at most, still to go before the rocky cradle of the beach, and then towards the jetty. I could see, across the bay, a boat making its way back to berth, a figure rowing within.

I swivelled back to Harriet. 'Let's rest here for a bit. Have some water, and then I'll get you home.'

From the rucksack I pulled a flagon and some rock cakes I'd taken from the biscuit tin. They were a few days old, but heavy and sweet, studded with currants, and Harriet bit down furiously on hers when I handed it to her.

'Harriet, don't be mad. It wasn't your fault; it was an accident.'

Harriet stared out to sea in glum silence.

'And don't be mad at me either.' She was wont to blame me when things went wrong on adventures that I had planned. 'That's not fair.' I didn't have to endure Harriet's silences often, but when I did they were awful. Cold and sullen.

She shifted her foot again, her eyebrows squeezing together. 'Why don't you go down and find those mussels, Kate. It's what you came for, isn't it? Leave me here. I'm fine. I'll watch you.'

None of this was said with any hint of warmth. Harriet obviously thought a fat ankle far too high a price to pay for fat shellfish.

I turned away from her and towards the sea. The little boat was getting closer to the end of the jetty.

'Fine,' I said. 'I'll go down and wait for that boat to come in. See if whoever's on it won't help us home.' I took the rucksack up but left the water beside Harriet. 'Call if you need me. I won't be long. Don't try to move.'

'I won't need you,' she said, and took a great bite from her rock cake.

TWENTY-NINE

The fisherman was still a distance away by the time I reached the tideline. A feed of mussels would mean the day wasn't a complete disappointment at least.

I headed across the black rocks, slick with bright green weed, and found a spot to perch where I could unlace my boots and peel off my stockings. The water was cold as I moved gingerly amongst the jagged shells, the slippery rock surfaces, the scuttling red crabs. I had to hitch my skirt high and tuck the hem into my waistband so as not to get it wet.

The purple-black mussel shells at the water's edge were not large enough for good eating, so I ventured further. The water rose to my shins, and I peered into the shifting shadows on the surface, searching for a plump bunch of mussels nestled in the crack of a rock. I bunched my skirt up further and bent down to roll my long drawers above my knees with my spare hand. I figured I had about ten minutes before I would have to cover up and ask for help.

Coming down the steps, I hadn't been able to identify the fisherman. Out in their boats, hats pulled low against the sea breeze, surrounded by their buckets and rods and lines, they all looked the same to me. It could be McPhail. I gazed back to the steps, where I could make out Harriet sitting. And what if it was him?

I turned back to my hunt. A few feet further out, down

at the base of one of the jetty pylons, I could see the dark shadow of a good bunch of mussels. I put my hand out to steady myself against the wood. From there I reckoned I could reach the crop, grab a great handful all in one go. My sleeves were going to get wet; there was no getting around that. I'd rolled them back past my elbow, but the water here was deeper, and I was going to have to give those shells a good tug to get them loose.

I bent towards the water and stretched down, my fingers long and white under the water, my arm going deeper and deeper. My hand was close now and, just as I reached lower still, a large crab ran across the mussel crop. I reared back, my foot shifting on the rock and starting to slip. I heaved my weight in towards the jetty, but it was too late. I tipped forwards, and my body submerged as I grasped to stop my fall. I squealed as I went under, the cold of it so sudden and soaking through my bodice and onto my skin. I scrabbled to get my footing and stood up, arms out away from my sodden dress, feeling water trickling down my back from the wet ends of my hair.

'Oh, oh, oh,' I exclaimed, cold and wet and indignant.

A shadow shifted across the water.

'Well, what have we 'ere?'

I raised a hand to shade my eyes, looking up at the shadow looming over the edge of the pier.

'Goin' swimmin'?' The figure stepped forwards, and I saw his face. It was Blackwell. He was smiling. And it was not a kind smile.

I turned away, conscious of my exposed legs, the sodden state of my dress.

'I'm fine,' I said. 'Thank you.'

'You don't look fine,' he said. 'Let me come down there and give you a hand.'

His footsteps thudded along the pier, away from me, and I clutched at my skirts, staring at the water I'd crossed, wondering if I could beat him to the shore and up the path before he got to me. I could see that Harriet, up on the cliff steps, was watching the little scene unfolding below her. Blackwell was hurrying down the jetty to intercept me on the beach.

I ducked my head into the shadow of the pier, trying to see if I could take a path through the rocks and weed and out onto the other side of the jetty, but there was no easy route. The sun glanced off the water, making it difficult to see. As I shielded my eyes, I noticed the dark shape of another boat coming in to anchor in the distance.

I looked back to the beach where Blackwell was approaching the end of the pier, and zigzagged my way through the slippery rocks towards the beach, aiming to the left of where Blackwell now stood. As I came closer to the shore, he wandered down, holding out his meaty hand.

'Really, you are too kind. I am fine,' I said, my arms crossed over my chest, letting my skirts fall completely into the water now, not minding the heavy drag of them as long as my legs were covered from his view.

'I insist,' he said. He left his hand outstretched.

I could smell the fishy stink of him. His thick-lipped smile was ruptured by rotten teeth. Again, I declined his hand, leaning away and attempting to sidestep him. I cleared the edge of the water and made towards the spot where I had left my boots. He moved faster, grabbing up my boots by the laces and clutching them to his chest.

'Let me,' he said, and crouched as if to kneel before me, holding my boots out as he did so.

I looked up at Harriet. She was still watching, one knee cocked as she kept the weight off her sore ankle. That damned ankle. I would never be in this position if it were the both of us down here together.

I moved back from him. 'Thank you, there's no need.'

'A man's only tryin' to help,' he said, as he shifted forwards on the rocky beach. 'Yer boots, m'lady.' He grinned and leaned in towards my legs so I could see the greasy shine of his skull through his hair.

Then I heard heavy footfalls, a voice calling, 'Blackwell!'

I turned and saw, striding down the pier, the figure of McPhail. There was an urgency to his steps that quickened my blood.

'Blackwell,' he called out again, insistent this time. 'Get away from her.'

Blackwell scowled as he stood, still clutching my boots. 'I was helpin' the lady out, McPhail. Nothing wrong with that.'

'No,' said McPhail coming up to stand to the side of me now, facing off against Blackwell. 'Nothing wrong.' And then he muttered darkly, 'But I doubt that's all you had in mind.' McPhail did not look at me. 'Give her back the boots.'

'I was just doin' that when you went and stuck yer nose in, wasn't I?'

The two men spoke only to each other, but every word they said was about me.

'Then hand them over,' McPhail growled.

Blackwell held out the boots, just short of me, so that I had to fully uncross my arms to grab them off him.

'You be more careful next time,' he said. 'Not very ladylike to fall in the drink.' He turned and walked towards the steps.

'Thank you,' I let out in a breath.

McPhail's jaw clenched. 'You shouldn't be down here alone. It's no place for girls, this.'

My skin prickled with shame. 'I'm not alone. I'm with Harriet. We came together, for the mussels, but she fell and hurt her ankle. She's on the path, just there.' I pointed up to where Harriet sat; she was watching the progress of Blackwell as he mounted the steps towards her.

McPhail spotted her. He took off across the beach, so that I was left hurrying to tie my boots and drag my sodden skirts and run after him, like a child. I caught up with him at the bottom of the steps.

'Harriet can't walk,' I called. 'Her ankle's too bad.'

McPhail didn't reply but tilted his face up to where Blackwell was approaching Harriet. We hurried up the steps towards them.

Blackwell's voice carried down. 'Yer waiting for your friend then, I s'pose? Feisty little thing, ain't she?'

'On your way, Blackwell.'

Blackwell turned to face McPhail as we came upon them. 'I suppose yer going to see these lovely ladies home, are yer? I'm not good enough t'smile at them. But you' – at this he stabbed a fat finger at McPhail's chest – 'you can see 'em all the way home and no one will bat an eyelid.'

McPhail stepped forwards; he seemed larger than usual. 'Be off, Blackwell – I'll not ask again.'

I kept in McPhail's shadow but inched around the step until I could reach out to grab Harriet's hand. I felt the charge coming off her.

'Yer not worth me while, McPhail. I wouldn't bother with blooding me knuckles on yer face,' Blackwell said, and he began to climb the cliff.

I offered a timid thank you to McPhail, at which he spun around to face us both.

'Don't be thanking me.' He almost spat the words at me. 'You've made a right fool of yourself getting drenched like that. If you were my daughters you'd be at home, helping your mothers, where you belong.'

Beside me, Harriet stiffened and clenched my hand.

'I'll get you to your horses and I'll see Harriet can ride. But you'll need to make your own way back. I'll not be responsible for either of you.' He set off away from us, leaving me to support Harriet and all her weight.

We shuffled up towards the top, both of us mute with shame.

'I slipped,' I said quietly to Harriet after we'd been struggling up the hill for a good while. 'I lost my footing and just went in.'

'I know. I saw. Don't take any notice of him.' She squeezed

159

my shoulder with her right hand, and I felt bad that she was comforting me, while she gritted her teeth through the pain of her swollen ankle and hobbled up the path towards the horses. 'He'll be sorry he's spoken so by the time we get up there and his temper's worn off.'

Harriet was not right on this occasion. The climb had not lightened McPhail's dark mood, and he waited by the horses, glowering.

I refused to be made to feel as if I were ten again.

'There was no need to wait for us,' I said. 'I'm perfectly capable of assisting Harriet onto Sadie. We've no need of your help.'

He glanced from me to Harriet. 'She won't be able to get herself up. I watched her come along the path – she can't put any weight on it. And you're not strong enough to help her into the saddle.'

'We've made it this far. Really,' I added with disdain, 'we do not need your help.'

I had no idea if I could get Harriet up on Sadie by myself but I would rather die than let McPhail know that. My clothes were drying tight and lined with salt across the contours of my body. I felt as though I had shamed us, and I did not like that he had made me feel this way.

He cocked his head to one side, keeping his eyes on Harriet, encouraging her, I suppose, to disagree with me, to implore him to assist us, but she did not. McPhail snorted and moved away from Sadie. 'As you wish,' he said.

Harriet leaned into me as we stood beside Sadie. When there was nothing to climb upon, we usually loosed the stirrups so that they hung low enough for us to get one foot in, pull ourselves up and then throw the other leg over. It wasn't the most graceful way, that was certain, but there was no need for us to be ladylike or ride side-saddle out on the cape. Sometimes, if we'd taken the horses without a saddle, I'd give Harriet a leg up, holding her foot or her knee in my laced fingers and hoisting her up so that she could swivel into sitting position.

McPhail had moved away but was refusing to leave our presence until he'd seen Harriet was safely on Sadie's back. I had to try.

'Kate,' Harriet whispered. 'I don't think we can do it.'

'We've done it before,' I said in my most soothing voice. 'You'll have to put your knee in my hands and I'll lift you. All you'll have to do is swing your good leg over.'

'Ouch!' she cried when we attempted it, and I shushed her. I didn't have the strength to raise her high enough.

McPhail called out, 'It is no trouble at –'

I cut him off. 'We are fine!'

We tried once more. Harriet bent her bad leg up and into my cupped hands and grasped the saddle, and I pushed the weight through my legs, propelling her up and off the ground. But she couldn't get into the saddle.

'Kate, it's no use. I'm too heavy. You can't.'

My face was aflame, my arms ached, and I could not look at her.

I heard her clear her throat and say evenly, 'Mr McPhail, if you'd be so kind …'

When I turned back I saw that McPhail had moved to Harriet's side. He excused himself quietly and then placed one arm around her waist and the other beneath the backs of her knees to lift her. The pale cotton of Harriet's skirt pushed between his fingers. I wondered if Harriet could feel the heat of his hand, the rough hardness of it, through the layers of cotton, branding her skin.

'Righto then,' he said, and without any effort at all hoisted her high onto the saddle, holding her there so that she could put a leg either side of Sadie's back.

She nodded to McPhail, and he nodded back. Did some understanding pass between them, or did I imagine that?

Ignoring me altogether he turned back towards the path

that led to the jetty, where his boat, and the catch he must have left behind in his hurry, would be waiting.

I was too cross to talk as we rode home. I did not know who I was more angry at: Blackwell for his vulgarity; McPhail for shaming me so; or Harriet for being so precious and twisting that damn ankle in the first place.

THIRTY

Harriet's ankle mended slowly, and she was fretful as she waited for the supply boat to bring the post and word from Melbourne and her beau.

When Captain Patterson did arrive, Harriet almost ripped the mailbag from the poor man's hand as he unloaded the crates.

'Waiting on a letter?' He smiled as he passed Harriet the canvas sack.

She rummaged through it and finally pulled out an envelope with her name on it, but realised at once it was not the letter she had hoped for. She held it up to me, and I recognised the handwriting.

'It's from Aunt Cecilia,' she said, deflated.

'Open it. She might have news of your Patrick?'

But, perhaps sensing the bad news contained within, she refused to read it in my presence and, insulted, I stomped off, taking the rest of the letters up to the station.

I located my father in the lighthouse from the rhythmic bangs ringing out across the station.

'Mail!' I called, as I ran up the steps.

He was attempting to shift a brass vent that was stuck. 'I'm making a racket, I'm afraid,' he said. 'But I'm glad to have some company.' He reached for the packet of letters I offered. 'What have we here?'

'I don't know, but Harriet was mightily disappointed with her lot.'

'Was she now?' he said, smiling gently. 'And why was that?'

'She was expecting a letter from her beau in Melbourne.'

'And it didn't arrive?'

'No.'

'Ah,' said Father, setting down the small pile he had rifled through, 'and nothing is as disappointing as a letter of love gone astray.'

We smiled together, and I asked if I might help him. It was pleasant to spend an hour or two working with him up in the light. There was less expectation on me than when I was working with Mother in the kitchen. There I was always adding too much flour, or had made the oven too cool or too hot. Each reproach from her suggested that she had failed in some way to pass down those kitchen skills and that I might forever be a disappointment if I could not master them. But with Father it was different. I was not required to know the arts of a lighthouse keeper and so it was easy for him to show me and for me to have a play at each task.

We worked together in companionable silence. Him, knocking the brass handle of each vent into place; and me, polishing the next one around with a rag.

'Did Harriet enjoy Melbourne, then?' he asked.

'Ever so much. The tales she tells, Father, of the grand buildings and the shops and the ladies in their finery.'

'Sounds as if you might also like to go to Melbourne?' he said, half laughing, so that I couldn't tell if he was being serious or not.

'Of course. But there is no one to have me, and Mother needs me here, does she not?'

Father banged twice, loudly in succession, and I paused in my polishing as I waited for his reply.

'She does. But these things are not impossible. There's some family in the country, down towards Melbourne. Some day, I suppose, we must arrange that you leave us for a time, even if it is to return as a wife and do as your mother did.'

I thought on his comment as I polished. But try as I might I could not imagine myself as my mother. I wondered what Father would say if he knew of Albert's proposal.

When I came down from the lighthouse and sought out Harriet, I found her inconsolable.

'Harriet! What is it?' I said as I kneeled down where she sat against the fence of the goat yard.

She turned her head away. I entreated her again and put my hand on her arm, and she thrust a paper at me and said bitterly, 'He has given me up! That is the news my aunt sends; he is to be married.'

'Oh, Harriet,' I said as I took the letter from her and scanned its contents.

It was true. Harriet's beau was to be married to a Miss Whitelaw in a winter wedding. Aunt Cecilia had told the news gently but practically, as it seemed there was no way around it. She expressed her surprise – and that of Melbourne society in general – at the announcement, but noted it was considered a good match by all.

'What a thoughtless man!' I said, sitting next to her and wrapping my arm about her shoulder. 'You are far better off without such a two-faced brute!'

Harriet lifted her face, which was all puffy with her crying, and wiped her hand across her nose.

'But he's not, Kate. He's perfectly lovely,' she said, and this started her off crying again.

All I could do was hold her shoulders and wonder how she might break the news to her mother who, I was sure, was already planning a wedding gown, and certainly not that of Miss Whitelaw.

To be spurned in love was a horrid thing, I saw this now. I felt a little tinge of remorse for the way I had treated Albert. We had hardly spoken since the bonfire. I could not imagine that he had shed any tears at my rejection, but I wondered if I had not been too harsh with him. I had not realised that, once

I could not turn over the bright little coal of his admiration for me in my mind, I would not feel so good about myself. I wondered whether it might have served us both better if I had encouraged his affection a little longer. I supposed that was as mean a thing as outright rejection, but certainly it would have given us both more pleasure than this cold ignoring of each other had.

I helped Harriet back to the cottage and quietly told Mrs Walker that there was unwelcome news in the letter. Mrs Walker's face fell, and she took a moment before she comforted Harriet. I wondered how many of her own dreams she had invested in her daughter.

My own mother seemed unsurprised when I relayed everything to her as we prepared the vegetables for dinner.

'She might have expected that of a city boy.' She handled the potatoes roughly and the peel shot off in all directions. 'Mark my words, they are not to be trusted.'

As I collected the peel in my hands and tidied around her, I wondered if anyone could be trusted at all, when it came to affairs of the heart.

THIRTY-ONE

Harriet was not to be relieved of her misery for almost a fortnight. I tried tempting her with walks, and then cake, and then treasures I found washed up on the beach. But she moped around and insisted that she was dying of sadness and that I should leave her be for she was terrible company. I began to agree.

Finally the day came when she smiled again, but it was not me who brought the smile to her face. No, it was McPhail himself who accomplished that feat.

He arrived just before lunch with a great sack slung over his shoulders and called out as he approached. The boys all ran to meet him and gathered around. Emmaline and I had almost finished hanging the washing, and she left the basket behind and skipped over to where they had all congregated.

I held back, for I still keenly felt the shame of McPhail's words down at Blackman's Bay and I'd wanted not to have to see him again for as long as possible. In addition, Albert had joined them all now. I hid myself amongst the flapping washing and hoped that I would get away with watching unseen.

I heard a voice behind me.

'Who are you hiding from, Kate Gilbert?' It was Harriet.

'What?' I said, startled, and then softened, for although she was on the mark, I was so glad to see her walking over to me, a half-smile on her face.

'You appear to be hiding amongst the washing – whoever from?' She raised an eyebrow.

'No one. I just don't care to race and see whatever it is he has brought in his sack.'

There were shrieks and yells from the children huddled round McPhail, who was holding open the sack.

'Looks exciting, whatever it is,' said Harriet.

'Hmmm,' I murmured in the most uninterested way I could muster. I felt her hand in mine.

'Come on,' she said. 'I need distracting.'

She pulled me away from the washing, and we met the little group as they came up the hill together. I could not help but wonder what it was she thought might distract her.

She let go of my hand as we neared them, and I dropped back, feigning interest in Edward, who was racing in circles around the group. I grabbed him and gave him a tickle so that I would not have to greet McPhail.

But the boy scrabbled out of my hands and yelled, 'Crabs! Mr McPhail has crabs for our tea!'

'Can we see?' said Harriet. 'Good morning to you, Mr McPhail.'

McPhail met Harriet's eyes. 'And to you. I trust your ankle is mending well?'

'Thank you, yes. Will and Harry, go and fetch a tin bucket from the laundry, will you, and we can put the crabs inside.'

'Wash the soap out first,' I called after them as they scampered up the hill.

It bothered me a little the way Harriet had come home and reclaimed her position of authority – I'd had to take care of all the children while she was off gallivanting in Melbourne. She bossed about the little ones when she chose, but also had been let off many of her duties these past few days while sulking over her broken heart. There had always been something of the princess about her, and usually I found it endearing. Lately, it had become tiresome.

By the time we got up to the verandah, Will and Harry

had pulled up a large tin bucket and half filled it with water. McPhail kneeled down beside it and released his hands from around the neck of the sack. He upended the whole thing into the bucket and there was a scrabbling, tinkering sound as the live cargo was dropped into the water.

Albert leaned in over the bucket. 'Gee, there's some fine ones there,' he said. He was getting nearly as tall as McPhail now and seeing their heads together, examining the crabs, I was filled again with shame and remorse remembering my behaviour with them both.

James drummed his fingers on the edge of the bucket. 'Which one's the biggest then, eh? He's mine.' Typical of my brother to want to be seen as the bravest. And just as typical the feeling that rose up in me.

'Only if you catch him first,' I said.

James scoffed at me. 'You won't put your hands in there. You'll get bit for certain.'

'No more likely than you,' I said, and there was a general *oooh* from those around us.

'Right then,' James said. 'You're on!' He pushed back his sleeves and squared off at me on the other side of the bucket. 'We'll take a turn each.'

The others moved back, and I kneeled opposite him, my shoulders straight so that I might feel as big as James.

'I'll even let you take first go – ladies first and all that.' He grinned and winked at Albert.

I narrowed my eyes at my brother. 'Lucy,' I said, 'will you count to thirty for me? When you get to the end my time is up.'

Lucy nodded at me.

'Careful how you go with them,' McPhail said, standing up as though to distance himself from our games. 'It's more than a nip if he gets you, and your mother won't be pleased if they're spoiled from your play.'

Harriet went to stand beside him. 'Can I fetch you some tea? I'll let Mrs Gilbert know you're here.'

My indignation was almost complete: Harriet wasn't even intending to stay and see my feat.

'Thank you,' he said, 'but wait till she's had her turn if you like. We might need a nurse on hand.'

'One, two ...' Lucy started to count.

I rolled up my sleeve and peered into the bucket; there were at least forty crabs in there. Some were smaller – Mother would surely scoff at their size – though a few, I could see, had shells bigger than my palm. It was one of them I needed.

'Make sure to grab him at the back, Kate,' Albert said, and James punched him lightly in the arm.

'I know that,' I said, irritated.

Albert didn't say another word.

I hovered my right hand over the bucket and began to lower it towards a large crab near the top. It was facing away from me, and I could see the two scarlet spots on its back where I needed to try and get my fingers. Just as I touched my forefinger to the top of the water, the crab scuttled to the side and lifted its large pincers. I snatched my hand back.

'Fifteen, sixteen, seventeen ...' Lucy counted on, and the boys laughed.

'Shush, you lot,' said Harriet. 'Go on, Kate.'

I pushed my knees in closer to the bucket and tilted forwards. I wanted that one. It had scurried nearer to the edge now and was cornered – exactly where I wanted him. I knew I had to be slow on the approach but quick and decisive when I grabbed so that the other crabs didn't latch onto my hand. I felt my teeth on the edge of my lip as I concentrated.

'Twenty, twenty-one ...'

Down I went, slow and steady. My thumb and forefinger at the ready. Then, quick as a flash, I darted my hand through the water and up and under the soft under-shell of the crab. I flipped him up and his pincers splayed in the air for a moment, but I couldn't get a good grip. He flew over the edge of the bucket and landed on the boards.

The others reared back, squealing, and Mother rushed out.

'What on earth?' she said as she saw us all there.

'Crabs,' said McPhail. 'For your tea.'

She took another look at us all crowded around the bucket and the poor crab scuttling with its pincers out to find a place to hide.

'Well, thank you,' she said. 'So they ought be in my kitchen and not out here playing games with all of you. Off you lot go.' She looked down at the escaped crab. 'McPhail, if you wouldn't mind bringing them in?'

'Of course,' he said, and bent down and scooped the loose crab up in one move and flipped him back into the bucket.

'Nearly had him,' he said to me, and I blushed.

James was complaining about not having his turn, and Will and Harry were already planning their own crabbing adventure.

I felt flustered. That I hadn't got the crab, that McPhail's eyes seemed to have already caught on Harriet's again, that I'd been short with Albert when I hadn't meant to be, really. I stood back and wiped my hands on my apron, ignoring James's snide comments as he went off.

McPhail picked up the bucket, and Harriet held open the door for him. He nodded at her, and she smiled and dipped her head in return.

Even though I was distracted, I remember the exchange clearly. And remembered it again, later, when I could bear to. For it was such a small moment, meaningless really, except that it was their last real encounter.

THIRTY-TWO

'Albert's grown quite tall, hasn't he?' Harriet didn't look at me as she spoke, just lay back in the sand and stared up at the clouds as I was doing, too.

'I hadn't noticed.'

'Surely you had, Kate.' She rolled over, and I could feel her eyes on me. 'Why, yesterday with the crabs – he is nearly as tall as McPhail.'

I did not like the direction this conversation was taking. I had yet to find the right occasion to tell Harriet about Albert's proposal – I knew I should because we had always shared everything. At first, I'd been too shaken from my scene with McPhail at the hut, and then she had received her own disappointment and I didn't have the heart to tell her that I'd had a proposal, when she no longer did.

'Boys grow so fast. James has shot up, too,' I said.

'So you have noticed?' she said, poking me in the stomach.

'Not really. Shall we go back?'

Harriet made no signs of moving. 'Patrick tried to kiss me, you know,' she said out of nowhere.

I sat up and looked at her with surprise. 'Did you let him?'

'Only for a moment, hardly at all.'

'Where?'

'We were in the garden at Aunt Cecilia's –'

'No,' I interrupted. 'On you. Where did he kiss you?'

She laughed. 'Oh, the neck, my cheek.'

'That's all?'

'A little on the lips.'

'What was it like?'

She rolled onto her back again. 'Lovely. It tickled a bit. But lovely.'

I thought about my dreams. 'Why did you not say before?'

She let out a sigh, as if I had asked a boring question. 'I didn't think you'd be interested. Or understand.'

I looked away, stung by her words. She thought herself so worldly now and considered me young and inexperienced. It did not matter that I was almost as old as she was. She had gone to Melbourne. She had been kissed.

'And now I shan't be kissed again until I convince Mother and Father to send me back to Melbourne,' she said.

'Surely we could find you someone on the cape to kiss?'

'Hardly!' she exclaimed.

'There's McPhail.'

She scoffed. 'You think about that often, don't you?' She stretched both arms in the air and then flung them out to her sides, so that her fingers rested near my leg. 'No, I rather think I'd prefer Albert to kiss me than the fisherman.'

I grew cold and hot at once. I didn't speak.

'Or *you* could always kiss me, I suppose.' She laughed.

My breath caught, and I coughed.

She ran her fingers up my leg and tickled me. I flinched away.

'Just for practice, of course,' she said and laughed again, that high, lilting laugh as though it were all such a joke and she could not see that my heart was somersaulting, and I was scarcely comprehending her first comment let alone able to take in her second. Yes – she could kiss Albert. Yes – I could kiss her. My thoughts all spun around and over each other, and my hands went to my heart for I was sure she must see it thudding through my dress. *Be still, Kate. Be still.*

I felt her eyes on me now. 'Goodness, Kate, I was only having a laugh – you look sick!'

'Albert proposed to me,' I said, not turning around.

Now it was her turn for surprise, and she gasped.

'When?'

'When you were away.'

'And what did you say?' she said, finally.

'I refused him.'

She was quiet again, as though she were running the past weeks over in her mind, recalibrating them with this new knowledge.

'You have kept secrets, too, then.'

I thought of the day fishing on the rocks, the ride down to McPhail's, my dreams.

'I told him no. I didn't think it was important.'

You lie, Kate Gilbert, Oh, how you lie.

'No,' she said, standing up and brushing the sand from her skirts. 'No, I suppose it's not.' She started back up to the path, and I followed her, and we didn't speak of it again.

The next afternoon I was taking the scraps out to the goat when I heard Harriet laughing. I stopped and turned towards the sound. She was sitting on the low stone wall near the lighthouse with Albert beside her. They had not noticed me, and so I watched them. Harriet swished her hair in the sun and bent her head in close to his, and she was so radiant, so full of all the attention she was paying him. Albert seemed transfixed; he was laughing, too, and they were sitting so close, so very close, barely a hand span between them.

I must have made a noise, or the intensity of my gaze must have penetrated into their shared consciousness, for they both looked up. There was a second where no one moved or spoke, and I held my breath. Albert's face appeared warm at first but, before my eyes, it grew hard and steely. He moved his hand from where it sat on the stone next to him and let it brush Harriet's, slowly, deliberately, and I saw it; he saw me see it. Harriet did not pull away.

I turned and fled, dropping the bucket behind me with a clank, hearing Harriet call my name as I tore down the hill away from them both. I flew so fast, my tears hot and blinding, that I would have been mown down by Dot and her cart had she not pulled her horse up short and called out.

'Whoa there, girl,' she said, and I wasn't sure if she meant me or the horse, but the moment of indecision caused me to slow down.

'Looks as though the devil himself is on your tail, lovey,' she said, peering out from under her wide-brimmed hat.

I stopped next to the buggy, breathing heavily.

'What's the hurry?' Dot pressed.

I avoided her gaze, looking up at the clouds scudding over the sun, its weak winter light smudged against the sky.

'Nothing, really.'

'It's the *really* that does the telling, my dear. Does all the telling.'

I scuffed my boots in the dirt.

'Whatever it is, dear, it won't feel this bad always, you know. Keep going then, don't stop for me.'

She gently tugged at the reins and started to move off.

'How long, Dot?' I suddenly called, my lips moving before I even knew what they were saying. 'How long does it take to not feel like this?'

She pulled up her horse and turned around so she could see me better. 'Well, everyone's different. But as sure as that sun will set and those waves will keep pounding these cliffs until they turn to sand, as sure as that, the badness you feel in you will pass. You just wait.' And she lifted the reins again and urged her horse on.

I considered the weight in my chest: Albert's and Harriet's heads bent in close together; Harriet's lilting laughter as she soaked up the attention; Albert's eyes as he moved his hand. Oh, how it hurt, so blindingly it hurt.

I walked the track aimlessly all afternoon, and as I walked, I fumed and cried and vowed that when I returned they would not know that I was upset at all. I was determined to lodge the feelings deep down inside me where they could do no more damage. Right down deep. Down so very deep they went, and I promised myself I would not even know they were there. Well, that's what I thought I'd done.

THIRTY-THREE

Perhaps it had all been for show. Harriet sought me out the next morning and would not leave my side. She did not know why I had run, why I was angry; she had been talking to Albert about me, I had misunderstood.

'I don't care, Harriet. Please stop speaking of it,' I said, and turned back to the mending pile.

The sock I was darning was scratchy and old, and the wool refused to lie the way I wanted.

I sighed in exasperation and threw the whole lot back in the basket.

'Let us finish this later,' Harriet said. 'Let's take a picnic together down to our beach.'

I was still mad. Mad at her and hurt, but I could see she was trying cheer me up. I thought of what I'd promised myself.

'Fine,' I said. 'The socks will have to wait.'

She took my hand and leaned in to kiss my cheek. 'Come on. Mother's made ginger cake. I'll steal us some.'

It had rained that morning, but now the sky was clear and blue. Wet leaves gleamed in the bright sunshine. Where the sun pooled on the track, steam rose from the earth. I breathed it deeply as we walked.

'Will you go back to Melbourne, do you think?' I asked after some time.

Harriet kicked at small stones, swinging the picnic basket

as she moved. 'I don't know, Kate. I so wish we could go together. Can you imagine it?'

I was quiet as I listened to her. She spoke of what we might see together, how we could have matching dresses made, and promenade along Collins Street arm in arm. She would have her aunt take me to the grand public library where I would see as many books as ever there were in the whole world, all there in one place.

'And we can go to dances,' she said. 'And you will have suitors, we both will, of course, and there will be parties and, Kate, it will be wonderful!'

I wondered if it would be. Yes, I wanted to see all of it, know all of it, but I wondered, as Harriet spoke, if it might not be the adventure I had always imagined it to be. Here was Harriet, after all, back from Melbourne, with nothing more than the fleeting memory of what might have been if her Patrick's intentions had indeed been true.

'Do you ever think we might be just as happy here?' I asked her, and she stopped and turned to me and put her hand out to stop me, too.

'No, Kate. We must go away – if we are to marry and have our own lives and families. There is no life for us here.' She was earnest as she spoke, in a way she had never been before. 'Remember all of those adventures you always wanted to have? The ones you read about. Well, you can have them. I know that now. There is a whole other world out there. It really exists.' She gripped my hand. 'You will adore it, I know you will. Why, you might do anything at all!'

We continued on.

'You know,' she said, 'there are women there who write books. I heard Aunt speak of them. They write books, or they teach. They are so clever, like you are.'

We walked down into a dip and the air grew a little colder as we crossed a small stream, come alive from the rain.

'Why,' Harriet was saying, 'if you still refused to think of marriage you could live with me and my rich husband who will look after us both, and you can write or read or do as you wish.'

I laughed with her. 'You'll still have to convince Mother to let me go,' I said. 'Perhaps when Emmaline is a bit older and James is old enough to help Father more.'

'They are old enough now. We should ask, today, as soon as we are back. Won't it be wonderful!' She shivered, and I didn't know if it was from the cold breeze or excitement. 'Look, there's McPhail's hut,' she said. 'Let's go and tell him! He can be the first to know of our adventure together.'

I had been so engrossed in our conversation I had hardly realised we had come to the place where the track forked down to our beach, McPhail's hut clearly visible through the trees ahead. I was surprised at her suggestion and had no desire to see him. 'I'd rather not.'

'Go on, let's tell him that we will both soon be leaving.'

'I hardly think he'll care,' I said, although I knew that he would care if Harriet were to leave again. I wondered at her sudden keenness to visit him when she'd been so reluctant that earlier time.

She pulled me along and, despite my resistance, I followed her. After a little way, Harriet stopped and put down the basket she carried. She gripped me by both wrists and spoke to me in that same earnest way again.

'Truly though, Kate, I do not want to go without you again. I missed you so.' It was as if she could not say this seriously enough. Her gaze was intense. 'You know that, don't you?'

'Of course,' I said. 'And I you.'

And she took my face in both her hands and leaned right into me, and her face was so close I could see the high pink of her cheeks, and the fine white hairs on her upper lip. Then she kissed me. Her lips were dry, and a puff of her breath, a little sour but warm, went straight into my mouth, and I closed my eyes and inhaled and opened them again. She was still there, and as her lips moved, ever so gently across mine, I was pierced by a feeling so acute I gasped, and felt her tongue, for a moment, just a moment, flicker against the inside of my lower lip. And then she pulled away.

'That is what it is like,' she said, smiling at me, as though it were the most natural thing in the world. 'That is what it is like to be kissed.'

I hold it, that memory, in a deep recess in my mind. I take it out and examine it, again and again and again. The light in it has grown old and worn; the features of her face, the colour of her hair are blurred now; but each time, it is like the first crack of a newly laid fire, the moment the flames begin to lick. The second that is not before and is not after but is only now and now and now.

Oh, Harriet, my Harriet, that we could have stayed there, that we had not gone forwards. That we had been content; that we had turned and gone home.

But we did not turn back. We walked on, me fervid with her touch and with the strange fantasy of Melbourne in my mind. We walked on to McPhail's hut to tell him our news, not caring if it sounded childish for we had such plans in our imaginations. We laughed and skipped. All my hurt at the previous day's events melted away as though it had never been, for who was Albert anyway, of what import was he when I had my Harriet, when she had me.

Happy and chatting is how we came upon McPhail's hut, and it barely dented our merriment that it was empty for we were as high as kites, playful and foolish, and we let ourselves in, as bold as you like, to take our picnic at his table, to drink his tea, to pretend.

THIRTY-FOUR

'Look,' said Harriet, as I undid our picnic things on the table. 'He has left his hat.' She placed it upon her head and growled. 'Who goes there in my hut?' Her voice broke, and we both erupted in laughter for she was truly hopeless, her voice so high and sweet that it could sound nothing like that of McPhail's or any man's at all.

'Here, let me try.' I took the hat from her and stood back, clearing my throat to deepen my voice. 'Why, come in, Miss Harriet, you look parched,' I said gruffly, and she laughed, stepping back towards the open door.

'Oh!' she cried dramatically. 'I couldn't, Mr McPhail. I am all on my own and it wouldn't do at all for me to take tea with you alone.'

I lowered my voice. 'Don't think of it, Miss Harriet, for you are quite safe with me.'

She backed further away, out the open door and into the light as I advanced, a leering grin on my face, and the hat pulled down low to shadow my eyes.

'Please, Mr McPhail, don't look at me so, for I am quite overcome!' She raised her hand to her forehead and threw back her head. Harriet in the sunlight. Picking up her skirts, a fistful in both hands, swishing them about, her hair slipping over her shoulders, a strand caught on her lips, as she turned this way and that, this way and that.

As I came to the doorway, I saw McPhail's rifle, leaning there against the wall. I took it up in both hands.

'I have ways of making you do as I say, young lady,' I growled in the make-believe voice, and held the gun in front of me. It was heavier than I expected and awkward, and Harriet's eyes widened as she gasped.

'You are very forward, sir,' she said, and lowered her eyes, peeking through her lashes and smiling.

Laughing, I raised the gun to my shoulder.

'Oh!' said Harriet and brought both hands to her mouth, her long fingers stretched over the O of her lips. She ducked her head, turned as though to run away from me, held up one splayed hand in mock horror.

There was a sharp crack. A bitter, burning smell. A shocking kick against my shoulder that spun me sideways so that I never even saw her fall. I dropped the rifle as I turned back. Saw a squawking flash of cockatoos go reeling and wheeling into the sky. The soft secret underside of their wings so close, so tender.

I heard a thud, cushioned by leaf litter, a strange gurgle of breath.

'Harriet.' My eyes told me one thing and my mind another, as if they were conversing in foreign tongues. I could not make what I saw and what I felt and what I heard and what I knew make any sense at all. *What a strange feeling,* I thought. *I must describe this to Harriet.*

'Harriet!' *It is part of the game, part of the scene,* I think. She has fallen, one arm flung dramatically away from her body, a white hand across her stomach, her legs tangled in her skirts; it's like a moment from a theatre piece.

Bravo, my love, I think, for we have never played like this before – and a slippery, dark thought, like a snake, sidewinds in the undercurrents of my thoughts. This is not a game. She is not playing. Something is wrong.

She has fainted, I decide. The shock of it. The cap has gone off. Somehow, I have fired the gun. I have frightened the birds and I have frightened Harriet, and she has fainted clean away and has crumpled to the ground there, and I shall hold her up and she shall open her eyes and blink and say, *Oh Kate, what an awful fright I have had. I thought that you had shot me.*

I take five steps and am beside her. I kneel down and slide one hand behind her shoulders and say softly, for you must always speak softly to one who has fainted, 'Harriet, Harriet. You fainted.'

But when I raise her up her head drops back, and her mouth gapes open and there is a wetness on my arm, a thick, warm wetness. Again my mind seems not to work for I cannot interpret what I see. I am firmer now; I am angry with Harriet for not having fainted because this is something else altogether but I do not know what. That snake again, glistening and black, sliding through my mind down to my chest, and it is looping, looping around my heart and squeezing and squeezing and, heavens, I am gasping, gasping, gasping. I cannot breathe.

Time unwinds. I am very still.

When we were young, I convinced Harriet to climb to a fork in the old gum at Murray's with me. She did not want to do it. I cajoled, I sweetened her up. I climbed slowly behind her, letting her feel my reassuring presence close on her heels, bracing for her if she fell.

Up and over the swirled knots of the gum we went, reaching around the white trunk to find a foothold. The only sounds, our leather boots against the grain of the tree, the heave of our breath as we climbed.

'Don't look down,' I told Harriet, and she did not, steadfastly, determinedly, going higher and higher, her eyes only on the next hand hold.

It was when we reached the fork that she realised how high we had come, how far below were the patchworked colours of the earth, the glinting surface of the sea. It was then that she froze, astride the branch, her arms hooked about the girth of the tree, and she whispered to me, 'Kate, I cannot move, I cannot move. Do not leave me here. Do not go.'

It grew dark while we were in that tree. I knew that I must go for help, to fetch her father, who could climb up and hoist Harriet over his shoulders if she could not be moved.

But every time I gently insisted that I would run, that I would run so fast she would scarcely notice me gone and that I would be back and we would climb down, she would grit her teeth and tears would choke her.

'Do. Not. Leave. Me. I cannot bear it.'

For hours we sat there. Hours while I spoke calmly and told her stories, recited great swathes of my favourite books, sang a hymn even, knowing that to climb down away from her would surely kill her.

It was late when the lanterns came moving through the bush, and the calls of the search party reached us.

'Up here,' I shouted. 'We are up here', and even when they climbed up and reached us, Harriet held me there with her strangled voice, saying, 'Do not leave me.'

She wept as her father carried her down. All the way down, I stayed close.

And when we got to the bottom, she clung to me and then she pulled away and yelled, 'I hate you! I hate you!' And buried her face in her father's chest and let herself be half carried home.

My own father took me kindly by the arm and walked with me in the dark hush of the bush. I ached with tiredness, my arms, my legs, my weary eyes and throat, and my father just led me forwards and didn't say a thing.

I am frozen here holding Harriet. She is not moving, and the dark pool is spreading below her head and it creeps towards my foot, and I shift the toe of my boot so that it doesn't touch and still I crouch here and still I do not move and inside my head I am screaming for help, I need help, I must get help.

I think I hear her voice, too, and I hear it say, *Do not leave me. Do not leave me here alone.* He will come, I think. He will come and find us here, and she will wake. He'll make her wake. She will sit up and shake her head and look at me and smile. And he will hold my shoulder and say, *There, there now, all's well.* Surely, he must come. The day is getting long, and the boats will return, and he will come, he'll come. He'll make it right.

It is only when I can no longer move my foot, when the sticky crimson pool has inched its way all around my black boot, and the sun is falling low in the sky that I know I must go. I lay her head down gently and stand, and my bones crack, and there is just that strange fallen expression on her face.

I fix her skirts and straighten her legs and say, 'I will be back so soon. I will run, I will run so fast and I will be back and everything will be well.'

The track disappears into the bush ahead of me, into those branches that will reach out like fingers to my face, the screeching calls of the birds, the shadows that will move and flicker and trick me. I am scared. I am so terrified.

I look back at Harriet and cry a little and say, 'Harriet, please don't make me go on my own.'

She does not answer, she does not move. I fall down next to her again and grab her hand and kiss the long cold fingers, and I *will* it, I *will* her to respond. I wish with every single breath, with every moment I have ever had, and every one to come. I say, 'Harriet, Harriet, please.'

But she is so still.

I turn and run.

THIRTY-FIVE

As I raced along the track the air grew cold, and my heart seemed to slow and harden inside of me. Those grasping branches scored red scratches up my arms, made foreign a path I knew so well.

When I paused to get my bearings, I thought of Harriet lying there by the hut and the dark pool that was spreading around her. An unearthly sound erupted from my chest and poured out of me, and I wanted to turn back, turn back everything and be in the moment before I lifted the gun, feeling it heavy and strange where it rested.

I ran and I tried to think only of running, of getting help. I ran against the panic that threatened to push me down into the leaves and stones and hold me there so that I was useless, so that I would stay there forever. I do not know how I made it back. Only that I did. That as the sun splashed the final light of the day across the cape, I came over the last crest of the track, and saw my father walking the boundary fence.

I called out to him, and he turned and raised his hand and left it there, just above his shoulder height, as though he suddenly saw something in me that foretold what was to come.

He began to move towards me, and I to him, so that when we met he caught me as I fell and held me upright on my feet, gripping me around my upper arms.

'Kate, for heaven's sake, what is the matter?'

How to tell, what to say? That black snake again coiling through my mind, and words hovering above me, out of reach, so that I stared at my father, pleading for him to understand from my eyes what it was that I had done. *Please, don't make me say it*.

'Kate!' He was firm now, and he shook me once, hard, so that my teeth clanked together and the words fell into place.

'I think I have shot Harriet.'

His face paled, and his lower jaw fell slack before he clamped it shut, the muscles below his ears visible as they twitched.

'Where, Kate? Where is she?'

'At McPhail's hut.'

A fleeting shadow passed across his eyes as though this place were both unexpected and inevitable.

'Quickly now,' he said, pulling me by the arm towards the cottages and shouting ahead as he did so.

'Walker! Walker!' I could see Harriet's father up on the hill, outside their cottage, bent over the verandah, his head down as he focused on a task. I resisted my father's pull, suddenly aware of what I had told, the news that was being borne ahead of me in my father's urgent tone.

Walker raised his head, and Father gestured wildly with his arm for him to come.

'Here, quickly,' he called. 'Get McPhail!'

And from behind the building a second figure appeared. My breath snagged, for it was him there at Harriet's cottage, his fishing sack in his hand. The two men looked at us, dropped what they held, and began to run. What a scene: they must have known as soon as they saw us. As soon as they noticed her absence. Something has happened.

Before they reached us, I saw the door open, saw the pale-blue swish of Mrs Walker's skirts as she stepped onto the verandah, curious at the noise. I saw her crane her neck, to work out where on earth we were all rushing to like this, this late in the day, with the darkness near upon us, the light to be lit.

I couldn't bear it. Fingers around my breath, my throat. I turned away.

My father's voice. 'Prepare for the worst, Walker.'

Harriet. Shot. McPhail's hut. We must hurry. The horses, get the horses. Calling now, back over his shoulder to anyone. Tell Albert he must light the lamp.

Walker, running towards the horses, leaping on Shadow and setting off. McPhail holding Blaze steady as he mounted and chasing after him, towards the hut, towards Harriet.

I had run four miles and I would have run it back again. But Father was by my side now, pulling me onto Sadie in front of him and holding me up as we sped down the track.

We heard Walker's calls as the hill evened out to the flat bush round the hut. My father yanked Sadie up hard and leaped down, leaving me behind as he ran towards the sound.

Harriet was no longer as I had left her but clutched in the arms of her father. McPhail standing to the side, gaunt and white, the rifle in his hand. As I approached I noticed the red-black blood across Walker's hand, on his shirt cuff, a smear across his forehead.

'She's dead,' he said to her, to us, to me.

THIRTY-SIX

It is hard to remember. I have tried not to for so very long. I buried it down deep and yet it comes. It rises to the surface in thin grey strands of memory. There are gaps. Great silences. Some moments so clouded by time and pain that I cannot see them at all, or what I can see is so confused, so disparate, that I believe it could not have happened that way.

The hours, the days, have all become as one. There is my mother's face, fearful and questioning, as though she is beseeching us to tell her it is not true. The hush that fell on the cape that night, as though the wind, the waves, the birds themselves had stopped for the shock of it. The sounds of Mrs Walker's grief. Emmaline and James, whom I glimpsed peering in through the kitchen door, where I sat wrapped in one of Mother's shawls, a nip of brandy in a glass in front of me; the expressions on their faces as if they were no longer sure who I was. As though they had finally seen what I had always suspected was lodged deep in me: something awful, something unspeakable.

An officer, a coroner, a jury from Edenstown came by boat. I watched them from the top of the tower where Father had let me hide, saw them arrive in their suits and hats and thought that Harriet would be so thrilled at the fuss we had caused. Dark thoughts slithered through my mind. The horizon seemed to tilt.

I remember Mrs Walker on the verandah with a red

woollen blanket. She held it clutched against her chest and then, when she got to the step, she stretched out both arms and flicked her wrists so that the blanket billowed out. I could not look away. She brought her arms back in and lifted it to her face. I wondered if she could smell Harriet. She put an arm out against the verandah post as if to steady herself. I saw her mouth open wide in a grimace, and her whole face was scrunched tight. Had she screamed like that I would have heard her. She was not screaming.

I could not know her pain. Only mine. But it was not yet pain – no, something else. I knew I had lost my best friend, my Harriet. Not lost her though. Killed. I had killed my best friend. Let the jury find that. Let them lock me up and call me a murderess. There is no harm greater than that I have already done. She is lost. And so am I.

They held the inquest on the third day. I remember the coroner was a man with a long silver moustache. He kept raising his left hand to smooth it down, from the centre to the edges, parting his thumb and forefinger. I thought of a seabird preening itself. I wanted to tell him, tell the jury about Harriet; that she did not like gingerbread but was happy with ginger cake. I wanted to tell them what it was to have her smile at you. I wanted them to know the smell, the rose-soap scent of her skin. I wanted to say we were going to Melbourne.

But they did not ask, and I could not say.

I remember Father and Walker being questioned.

Walker was called first. He said Harriet and I were the best of friends. He said he had arrived with my father and McPhail and found the body where I described. There were no signs of struggle. It was an accident, he said; he was sure of it.

When Father was summoned he said there were no bad words between us, that there was a bloody wound to the back of her head. I thought about cradling her head while the earth around me grew dark. I thought about her hand splayed up and the surprise in her face. Then I could not think anymore for it was my turn.

They asked me so many questions. I told them I took the gun and held it up. I did not fire. I did not mean to fire. I did not remember the gun going off. I did not remember checking the catch. I did not remember hearing the gun. I told them we were the best of friends; we were playing, is all. There was nobody else there. I ran all the way home.

Then McPhail was up, and he said he was a fisherman, that he'd got some mullet that day and brought the catch up to the settlement. He identified his gun, said that he kept it at home, loaded with small shot. That he always kept it capped. He said he knew us, and that we were very close.

When they called on the doctor, he said that the wound showed the gun had been only inches from the back of her head to make such a mess.

I thought about inches. I thought that couldn't be right. I thought about the doorway, and Harriet, in the light. Her smile, the way her head turned. My fingers on the trigger. My Harriet.

I no longer knew what was true.

I remember them sending us out as they deliberated, and I sought out a spot to hide where no one would speak to me.

I overheard Mrs Jackson talking to Mrs Walker.

'More tea?' Mrs Jackson said.

'Thank you.'

'It's a terrible thing you have to sit through this.'

I wished that I could close my ears.

'It must be done,' said Mrs Walker.

'She cannot be allowed to go unpunished,' said Mrs Jackson. 'I'm sorry, but I must say it. Perhaps it was an accident. But that girl must pay.'

Mrs Walker's voice was weary when she finally spoke. 'Kate has lost her, too. Please,' she said, 'let us not talk of it anymore.'

'What will they do to me?' I whispered to Father when we had all been assembled once more in the parlour.

Mother rubbed my arm. 'Hush now,' she said as though I were her baby again.

I remember the way the foreman stood and announced that they had made their decision. I slid the nail of my right thumb under the nail of my left and I pushed until I felt the skin tear.

'And what is your finding?' the coroner asked.

'That Harriet Walker, aged seventeen years, died of a gunshot wound to the head, accidentally received –' My mother gasped. 'Accidentally received,' he said again, 'and that her companion, Kate Gilbert, was not to blame, as they were skylarking.'

In my head clouds of cockatoos lifted into the sky, wheeling and crying.

THIRTY-SEVEN

I went to my bed and I stayed there. All the rest of that day and the next. The world of the cape went on past my window. I thought I heard Harriet's voice drifting in but, of course, I did not.

Then, on the fifth morning after it happened, my mother pulled back the covers, gently but firmly, and forced me to sit.

'You must pay your respects, Kate,' she said.

I was still in the same clothes from the inquest, but she didn't comment, just smoothed back my hair and led me down the hallway and out the door and across the grass to the Walkers' cottage.

I faltered at the step, tugging back against Mother's grip.

'I can't,' I whispered, my voice cracking.

'You must, Kate. She will be buried today.' She let me lean against her as we went up the verandah stairs. She knocked softly on the door.

Walker came and dropped his head when he saw us but moved aside. I heard a swish of skirts as we entered and looked up to see Mrs Walker crossing the end of the hallway.

Mother said 'Annie', but there was no reply. It was cold, so cold in there. The fires must not have been lit. My whole body shook.

Mother pushed me down the hall towards Harriet's room, and I tried to resist, for I could not go in there. But she pressed her hands against my back until we reached the door. Mother opened it, and there, laid out in her best blue dress, was Harriet.

There was a sharp smell in the room – peppermint – masking something else, something foul. It did not smell as it had in all the days that Harriet and I had lounged together on that bed.

Mother crossed herself. She stepped forwards and kissed Harriet's cheek. Then she turned to me. 'Sit, if you'd like.'

I shook my head, but my mother fetched a chair from the corner and placed it level to Harriet's waist.

'I'll just be outside,' Mother whispered, and I gripped her arm as she made to leave but I could not take my eyes from Harriet. Mother unwrapped my fingers, patted my hand and left.

It was Harriet, and yet it was not her. Without animation, without life, her face was unfamiliar. She wore a bonnet. White and trimmed with lace. The lace wound down beneath her chin and was tied there. I could not see my Harriet, with her golden curls flying, tumbling, framing her face. Her eyes were closed. Her skin so pale. Around her wrist was a white satin ribbon. I reached out to place my fingers on it and, at my touch, the bow came apart and slid into my hand. Startled, I took it and held it to my face.

I breathed deeply. Scrunched the ribbon and breathed in again. It did not smell of her. When had Harriet ceased to live, when had that smell of hers been washed away? Had her mother washed her clean? How had she managed it? How had she held Harriet as she moved first one limb and then another? It was too much to think about. I stuffed the ribbon in my pocket and leaned forwards to kiss her cold forehead. Not because I wanted to, but because I felt I must.

This was not Harriet. I had killed her.

I left the Walkers' cottage and returned to my room without a word.

They buried her without me. Mother and Father said it was best. It would be too upsetting for me. And by that, I knew they meant for Mr and Mrs Walker. They could not look at me. I understood.

I lay on my bed. Even though I knew they were too far away for me to hear – down in a little clearing in the bush, near our cove – I sensed the wind carry the hymn to me. Up through the trees, along the track, over the point and the yards, all of which had been ours. All ours.

Heav'n's morning breaks, and earth's vain shadows flee;
In life, in death, O Lord, abide with me.

I turned to the wall. I closed my eyes.

THIRTY-EIGHT

It was a month before I got away from the cottage, creeping out, avoiding the anxious faces of Mother and Father, and dashing into the shelter of the bush where I could hide in the shadows. It was a cool day, but I felt clean in the air, blowing as it did through my hair that had grown matted and stale as I lay, day after day, in my room.

As I hurried from the cottages, I thought I heard my name called, but I dared not turn around. It was only ghosts who spoke to me now, and I was not yet ready for what Harriet's ghost might say.

I wandered without thinking. Trying to let my eyes fill with the familiar sights, but everything, everywhere was Harriet.

I did not mean to end up at the hut. It was only when I smelled the bitter wood smoke that I knew I was close. I came upon the track, and then the door, and I knocked.

There was the sound of a chair pushing back across the floor. Soft padding feet. McPhail opened the door. For the longest time he did not speak. It seemed as if he might just turn away. But then he stood back and swept his arm towards the room. I stepped across the threshold.

'You're cold,' he said.

'No.'

'Tea?'

'Yes, thank you.'

He motioned for me to sit and moved to stand over the billy on the stove. The water boiled; I could hear it roiling and spitting.

'The tide is high this morning,' I said.

'Yes.'

'The catch?'

'So-so.'

'You'll bring it up?'

'Perhaps.'

He picked up the billy. Pinched the black tea leaves inside. Poured the steaming water. Turned it once, twice, three times. Again he did not ask how much sugar I took. I watched the granules fall as he spooned it in. Three spoonfuls. Strong and sweet.

My eyes moved around the hut. Skipping to the shelf, to the scratched surface of the table, drawn inevitably to the corner, where the gun had sat.

'The gun?'

He raised his eyes to mine. 'They took it.'

'Of course.'

I reached for the cup he offered me. My hand was shaking so much that hot tea splashed up and onto it. Putting the cup down, I drew my hand instinctively to my mouth and sucked the fleshy part between thumb and index finger that was already glowing red.

'Cold water,' he said. 'Here.'

He grasped me by the elbow, helping me stand and move towards the stove, to the bucket beside it filled with rainwater. He guided me to kneel down and plunged my hand in the cold water. He held me by the wrist. My sleeve wet to my elbow. I cried out at the pain of it.

'It will stop the burning.'

'I'm sorry,' I said, and I didn't know what I was saying it for.

'It's no matter.'

'No.'

We crouched there. He and I. By the stove, by the bucket. I felt the heat leaching out of the burn.

'It was an accident,' he said.

I began to cry. I could not stop. He did not ask me to. I could not look at him. I was bursting, falling, dying.

He removed my hand from the water and lifted it to his mouth. He placed his lips on the burn. He closed his eyes.

His lips were dry. Rougher than my own. Than Harriet's. I found that my tears had ceased. While his eyes were closed I could look. There was a deep crease across his forehead, as though it were an unbearable thing he was doing. As though it were causing him pain.

I wondered if he'd ever had the chance to do this to Harriet. If she had kept more secrets from me. I was sure he had wanted to touch her like this. I'd no doubt that he had imagined this and more. Fingers on button-holes, lips on the neck.

But this was mine now. An ache strummed between my hipbones and fizzed in the pit of my stomach. Like a pinprick of light, intense, so bright.

We crouched there for a long time, McPhail and me. His lips on my hand. I leaned over the bucket and lifted my other hand to the side of his face. His beard was thick and scratchy. He groaned in his throat and inclined his head towards my hand, so that I was cupping the arc of his chin, my fingers stretching up towards the lobe of his ear.

If I do not speak, I thought, we might stay like this forever. This man, this grown man, was trembling at my touch. I feared he would begin to cry and I would not know what to do. But now, for now, I knew everything.

He opened his eyes. They flashed.

'Harriet,' I said, dropping my hand. 'You think of her.'

'No,' he whispered, but he could not hold my gaze.

I turned my face away and closed my eyes. 'I think of her, too,' I said. I think of nothing else. Harriet twirling in the light, laughing, hair slipping over her shoulder. Harriet's face so close to mine, her kiss.

I stood. 'I will go.'

There was a thunderous pounding on the door.

'Open up, McPhail! I know your game!'

'It's Albert,' I whispered.

The voice was clear and angry. The banging louder now.

'I'm coming in!'

McPhail got up; in his haste he knocked the bucket with his knee and water slopped over the edge and onto the floor. Before he had a chance to move to the door, Albert flung it open and stood there, silhouetted against the pale light.

'Kate, come with me,' he said, striding across the room to where I now stood and grabbing my arm. I shook him loose.

'Watch yourself, boy.' McPhail took Albert by the shoulder.

Albert, enraged by the touch, turned on McPhail, striking out. It was odd. I remembered what Harriet had said – what I had also noticed. He was the same height as McPhail. Smaller in stature, but strong.

'Have you not done enough?' Albert shouted. 'Do you mean to ruin them both?'

McPhail froze, then lurched forwards, grabbing Albert by the shirtfront with both hands. He roared into Albert's face, a wordless roar. I had to look away.

The small room echoed with the sound. When I turned back it was to see McPhail pushing Albert away, crossing the room hurriedly, grabbing his coat and hat, and walking through the open doorway. He did not look back.

We both watched him go.

'You need to come with me now, Kate,' Albert said. He reached his hand out again and, this time, I let him take me by the elbow, lead me out the door, shut it behind us.

When we had moved a few feet from the hut, Albert dropped my arm and turned to face me.

'I saw him touching you.'

I was silent.

'I did. And I want to belt the man.' At this Albert clenched his fists by his sides, and I could see him gritting his back teeth together. 'But I am prepared to forget what I saw. As long as he leaves and does not return.'

Over Albert's head the gums were rustling and whispering against the grey clouds.

'It was nothing. I burned my hand.' I held it out towards him, and he glanced at the red mark, fainter now, but visible, as if I'd been branded.

He stepped towards me and took my hand in his. 'Why were you here?'

How could I tell him when I did not know myself? Because of Harriet. Because of McPhail. Because there is a great weight in my chest and I cannot breathe for it. Because no one is angry at me but no one can look at me. Because I killed the person I love most in the entire world. Because I did not mean to.

Because sometimes I think I did.

'I walked. I was cold. I saw the smoke. He made me tea.' I wasn't making sense.

Albert cocked his chin, turned away from me, turned back. 'Have you thought more on what I said that day?'

'What you said?'

'What I proposed.'

'What?' I laughed bitterly. 'Marriage?'

'Yes.'

'You do not mean it.' I pulled my hand away and began walking towards the track.

'I mean it, Kate. I still want to marry you. I would marry you. You should consider it.'

All the fear and guilt that was curdling away inside me came foaming up. 'Why?' I shouted. 'Because no one else will marry me now?'

'I never said that.'

'You didn't need to.' I took a deep breath, looked him square in the face. 'You shouldn't have followed me here, Albert.'

'I was worried about you.'

'Don't. I will be well soon enough.'

'Will you think on it?'

I did not reply.

His face, the softness there. There was something in him that gave me peace. He was right. I could marry him. No one else would have me now, not anyone who knew, anyway.

'Will you see me home, please?' I asked.

'Of course.'

Tenderly, he took my elbow, and we walked back to the track. Not fast, not slow. At some point he began talking of the vegetable garden, the supply boat that had come a week late because of a storm, the younger boys' escapades trying to catch crabs. I listened and nodded and felt his warm hand on my arm. Where McPhail's touch had scattered me – blown me into millions of pieces so that I could focus only on the tiniest points, the pressure of his lips on my hand – now I felt centred. I felt as I had before. I was walking with Albert and he was talking and the light was changing and the birds called *curlew! curlew!* in the treetops around us and it could have been any day from my past.

Perhaps Albert could remake the world for me. Perhaps it would be easy to pretend with him. Perhaps, in time, we could move away from the cape and find ourselves a little house, and I could tend to it and he could find some work, or we could go to the city or follow the gold and perhaps, in time, I might be able to breathe again.

I might forget.

THIRTY-NINE

It rained incessantly for weeks. Rain that brimmed over the gutters and fell in sheets so that I had no choice but to remain inside.

Mother ushered me from my room early each morning, so that I wouldn't sit in there all day feeling sorry for myself, she said, and we spent our days in a kind of a fervour of busyness: cleaning the store cupboard and house; baking breads and teacakes so that the oven roared with heat, and we sweated in the kitchen despite the icy rain outside.

I hadn't been down to the beach or past the hut again or ever to the grave, for I was trying desperately to keep myself in the present, the future, to find a way forwards and out of this. I was leaving soon on the next supply boat. Bound for Bendigo, for six months with my father's distant cousin, whom my parents had begged to have me, to get me off this godforsaken cape and see if I could shed the grim shroud of my recent past.

No one on the cape had made me feel as though I had to go; Albert had been persistent in his kindness, and I ached to be able to let this kindness wash away all the tumult that I felt, but there was this weight in my chest. A cold heaviness that I did not know what to do with. I could not feel anything other than its presence there.

One morning I had woken to the wind, only the wind with no rattle of drops on the tin roof. I was up and away before anyone had the chance to stop me.

I knew the grave was some way from the lighthouse, in a little clearing that one could reach from the track. Far enough away to not make Mrs Walker desperate with grief, close enough for her to take the walk each day. It was marked simply by a white cross inlaid with a heart-shaped plaque. Her name, the dates, a poem.

Oh, we miss her and how
Sadly bleeding hearts alone can tell
Earth has lost her
Heaven has found her
Jesus doeth all things well.

As I stood beside the grave for the first time, I was filled with a mixture of sadness and guilt and selfish, selfish pain at my loss. I questioned whether Jesus did indeed do all things well, for this felt like a terrible mistake. If Harriet had always been intended to be taken up early to serve her Heavenly masters, why, then, did the invisible hand of fate not choose to wash her from the rocks, have her fall from a horse and snap her neck, be bitten by a treacherous brown snake slinking across her path? Why, dear God, in all your infinite wisdom, did it have to be by my hand? My jealous hand, moved at times by an energy I felt came from outside myself.

I kneeled down beside the cross and wiped my hand across the face of the plaque. In truth, it was not because I had been so racked with grief that I could not bear to come, but because I was terrified of communing with Harriet in the afterlife. What could I say that would ever recompense for what I had done? Not that she could hear my innermost thoughts, the ones that whispered: *You meant to do it. You meant to pull the trigger. You're better off without her. You would always be second to Harriet.*

I was terrified that when I kneeled down to pray, to confess, the words would gurgle up from the depths of me, and my true self would be revealed in all its duplicity.

'Harriet?' My voice came out croaky at first. 'I am sorry not to have visited till now.' I folded the hard little hem of my apron in my lap, turning it over, and over again.

'I am leaving the cape.' The wind whipped in the treetops above me, and I glanced up at the noise, pulled my shawl in tighter around myself. 'Just as you said.'

Every word I spoke was wrong. Should I try to explain how sick with guilt I was? How I would never, ever forgive myself?

'I don't know what to say to you, Harriet. So I'm just going to start talking. Your mother is well. I mean, she's not well, she ... survives, I suppose. But she is out of bed this week. She and Mother are both seized by this need to scrub and clean everything down. As though we have, all of us, been soiled somehow by the accident.' At this I hesitated. 'Your death, I mean.'

I startled at a cracking noise behind me. When I swung around, I saw nothing but the dense bush for a moment, and then, there, stepping through the trees, was the black girl. Had she followed me? I stood up. She wore the same thin skirt as before but had discarded the scrap of waistcoat for a man's shirt. Her feet were still bare. Why was she here and why show herself now? She looked at me and past me to the grave. I remembered the last time I had seen her, high on the hill, in the heat, as I watched the supply boat leave, with Harriet on it.

It started to rain again, a thin drizzle, misting through the trees. I could feel the drops beginning to bead on my forehead and drew my shawl over my head, not daring to turn away from the girl who watched me. She motioned for me to come. Her head inclined, her shoulder turned. An expectation that I would follow. I realised with a start that I had often made the same motion to Harriet. Not waiting, just expecting. An arrogance of sorts, a pride.

I did not want to stay there by the grave, and I did not want to go home. I followed, under the now dripping ti-tree across the swathes of slippery bark that had fallen from the tall eucalypts. She walked ahead of me, and she did not look back to check that I was there. Just moved through the bush, following no track that I could see.

I turned once and wondered how I would find my way out. Perhaps it was better that I became hopelessly lost. That I did not make my way home. I was no use to any of them anyway. I was broken. The only thing that had made me feel anything in the month since Harriet's death was the burning touch of McPhail. I craved it. Oh God, how I yearned to feel something again.

The girl had stopped. She waited until I was close behind her, then moved ahead a little into a copse of banksia trees. It was darker in there, shadowed by the layers of twiggy bare branches, but sheltered from the rain. She moved to stand before me. She was just the taller. I wondered how old she was, how close in age to me. To Harriet.

When I had seen her before, I thought that her boldness came from her ease with her body, the way she stood with her shoulders back and her breasts barely covered. But it was not that, for now she was dressed as I might be – shabbier than me, true, but essentially the same. It was the boldness in her presence. As if she were challenging me. Questioning me.

She reached one hand out towards me, and I shrank back. She paused, but when she saw that I did not retreat again, she moved forwards and placed her hand on my chest, on the exact spot where I felt the great weight. Her hand was warm through the damp fabric of my dress. She did not look at me but began to speak. Her voice was low, her language a cadence that was not like the harsh calls I had heard before. It did not sound so foreign to me here, as though she were singing the words of a lullaby that I couldn't understand, but I knew was meant to comfort me.

She stopped speaking, raised her hand and tapped it against my chest, once, twice, and lifted her chin.

'It is like a rock,' I whispered, knowing that she probably could not understand. 'Like a great weight I cannot move.'

She did not draw her hand away. Instead she took my own hand with her other and laid it on her chest. I could feel the faint thud of her heart. She held my hand there, but she needn't have, for I did not want to pull away. She looked at me, her eyes steady on mine. As though she could see into me completely. As though she could see the rotten foulness of my interior, all the guilt and the grief and then back further to the envy, to the lust and jealousy. Still her hands remained, one on the great weight in my chest and the other holding my hand against her heart.

She began to speak again, but this time it was only noise, as if there were no words but only a mournful, calling wail. Where her hand lay on my chest I felt warmth spreading and imagined that it was curling in through my skin and its long tentacles were twining around the rock inside of me and finding invisible fissures. She sang, and I felt the warmth begin to crack the rock, letting the light in, and the air in, so that at its very core it was not solid anymore and, as we stood there, hand to chest, the song wound around me and the rock gave an enormous crack so that I gasped and it exploded, exploded all around me in light and I could breathe.

I could breathe again. I took in great gulps of air and wept.

FORTY

I sat in the tower with my father the night before I was to leave, and I did not know what to say. Nor did he. He began, and stopped, and began again, but nothing felt right to him, it seemed.

I wanted to tell him that I didn't mind. That it was enough to be back up there in the tower, the light shining out above us, feeling high and separate from the world. Knowing the waves would roll in and roll on forever, that the light would stand sentinel. Blink, flash, blink.

I stepped out onto the balcony, and the wind whipped my hair across my eyes. I raised my hands to my ears so that they didn't fill with the whistling cold.

The moon was nearing full, and the cape was spread below us in silvery light. The moon shadow of the lighthouse pointed across the scrub out to the sea in the direction in which the boat would take me tomorrow.

Nestled in behind us were the three cottages, a faint glow in the windows, three plumes of smoke, rising up and being taken by the wind. Inside ours, my mother, my sister and brothers would be going about their night-time duties. My siblings were relieved, I imagined, that I would be gone. That they might finally escape the brittle edge of emotion I had brought into our home. Mother would take it harder. But she, too, might breathe easier with me gone for a time, knowing that she and Father had set me on a path from where I might recover something of a life. Do my duty to the family. Marry.

In the smallest cottage, Albert would be reading to his younger siblings. He was a good brother and kind. At his pressing I had agreed that I would consider his proposal while I was away. That I would come home six months hence with a final answer. He had taken my hand in his and said I must promise to do this. And I said I would.

I would not marry Albert. I knew it then, but I could not bear to cause any more hurt before I left. I had told him to keep watch over my sister and brothers for me. I hoped, perhaps in time, that he might draw close to Emmaline. That she might bring him happiness.

There, too, was the Walkers' cottage. I could not see the emptiness that existed without her, but I knew it was there.

A few days ago, when Mother and I were packing, I came upon my shelf of books, Harriet's books, and I was suddenly filled with dread. I had not turned a page for months, but I could not imagine leaving without the company of those great friends.

Mother noticed me hesitate and said, 'Oh, Kate. You must return them to Annie. They are Harriet's, after all.'

'I suppose I must.' I took out *The Coral Island* and ran my hand across its cover. Mother moved over to me, and I felt her hand on my shoulder.

'After George …' she started, and I hushed her.

'Mother, you do not have to explain.'

'But I do, dear Kate. It is just that those things that were his were all I had left of him. I could not let them leave my sight.'

'I understand,' I said, and piled up the books and asked Mother to see them returned to Mrs Walker. I thought it best I didn't go myself.

Standing out there on the lighthouse balcony in the wind, I recalled how, just yesterday, holding little Lucy's hand on the way out to feed the goats, I'd suddenly felt a wretched tug right in the soft place where my rib cage met. It was the feel of her fleshy hand in mind. All those ridges of skin coming against each other, pressing sweat and warmth and feeling. I thought of all the times Harriet's hand had been in my own. I thought of how it was always her palm turned forwards towards mine, mine back towards hers and if, for some reason, we mixed this up, it felt so strange we pulled our hands apart, fumbling and laughing, until we had righted them and carried on.

I wondered, perhaps for the thousandth time, why I had not lain down beside Harriet at the hut and taken her hand in mine and not moved until they had come and found us. Why I had not recognised that I would never hold her hand again, and that holding it as it grew cooler and cooler until it was cold would have been a comfort, at least to me.

My father called from inside the tower. 'Don't get too cold out there.'

'Coming,' I replied and turned my head to look down further. Past the cliffs to our beach, and tucked back behind it to where I knew the hut was.

I had not seen McPhail again. Father had said that he had gone north and would be away for some months. He did not stop past to say goodbye. For this I was glad. I could not bear the thought of him near. I dreamed of him, of Harriet, and I woke in feverish sweats and rubbed at my eyes until I could no longer see the haunted visions in my head.

A cloud scudded across the sky, shadowing the moon, until it reappeared, bright, illuminating the cape once more.

I looked towards the bush that hid the clearing where Harriet lay.

'I am sorry I am leaving you,' I said to the wind, 'but I have to go from here.'

I ducked back in through the door to the warm lantern-light of the tower, and my father saw me down the steps and said I must sleep now for there was a long journey ahead.

Mother embraced me and held her lips against my cheek.

'See that you send word as soon as you're settled.'

'I will, straight away,' I said as I moved out of her arms.

The children had already kissed me and were running up the hill so they could watch me leave from the cliffs. Albert had chosen not to come down to the jetty.

Suddenly there was a shout from the track, and Walker was there. 'Wait!' he called out.

I looked at Mother, anxious now to be away, not to prolong these goodbyes.

Walker was breathless as he approached. He held a package in his hand and pushed it towards me.

'Annie wanted you to keep this,' he said as I took it in my hands. Rectangular and heavy. One of the books. 'She knew it was your favourite. Harriet' – at her name he stopped, unable to go on for a moment – 'Harriet always said.'

I thanked him, and he placed one hand on my shoulder and squeezed, just for a second.

'Go safely now,' he said.

I hugged Mother one last time, and then Father helped me down onto the boat.

From the stern I watched the cliffs grow smaller. I waved and waved to the group at the top of the cliff. I saw Emmaline, holding Lucy's hand, keeping her safe back from the edge. In a trick of the light I thought I saw them throw their hands up to the sky. I thought I saw Harriet and me, standing on top of the world, of our cape, laughing and brave and fearless in the face of the lives ahead of us. So great and unknown.

I felt in my pocket for Harriet's ribbon. I drew it out and fingered the soft satin and brought it to my lips. I held it up and waved again, and the ribbon trailed out in the wind and twirled and swirled, and I saw the girls jump and wave both hands in the air.

And then I let it go. It spun up for a moment in an eddy of wind and then whipped up and away. I watched it against the flurries of white caps, against the blue sky, the racing clouds. Then it was lost, and I could see it no more.

The cliffs grew more distant, and I turned to look at what lay ahead. Captain Patterson stood at the prow, scanning the horizon.

'Alright there, miss?' he called back.

'I am,' I said.

EPILOGUE

Had I known what was to come, would I have felt so light, so free, with every mile I travelled away on the boat that day? I thought I had experienced everything, lived it all in those years on the cape, but I knew nothing of the love and the loss that lay ahead of me. I did not realise that I would step off the boat onto a jetty that led to a road that led to a city and eventually to a man and babes I would bear and then lose as men in the filthy foreign mud of a land I would never get to see. That, as happens, one thing leads to another and to another. Good or bad. Joy or sorrow, there is so little about it that we can control. It is fate, damn destiny, that has its way with us.

Oh, to remember. It is sweet and bitter, both. To remember it all has filled me with the vast light of the cape again, allowed me to feel Harriet's hand in mine once more, bruised me with grief. I often return to that day in my darkest hours, to the doubt that haunts me still, the moment – again and again and again – when the gun goes off, when she falls.

Forgive yourself, I have sometimes imagined I hear her whisper in the wind. For that is what she would have said. And, perhaps, when the day comes for my redemption, not so long away now, I will find that I have.

What I lost – what was elusive – in all those years of trying not to remember, was the truth: about her, about us. She made me, is always part of me. For all that came after, for every other moment that has plucked at my heart or made it sing or broken it, there was never a time, never a love, like that.

Harriet, my Harriet, my love.

AUTHOR'S NOTE

Skylarking is a work of fiction, based on the true story of the accidental shooting of Harriet Parker by her best friend, Kate Gibson, in the hut of Donald McPhail at Cape St George in 1887. I came upon this story while camping with dear friends near the site of Harriet's grave at Greenpatch camping ground in Jervis Bay, New South Wales.

For my research on the true story of what happened at Cape St George, I am indebted to Bridget Sant's work *Lighthouse Tales: Intrigue, Drama & Tragedy at the Lighthouses of Jervis Bay*. I have explored a number of lighthouses during the writing of this book and am grateful to staff and volunteers at the lighthouses of Point Hicks, Cape Schanck and Cape Otway for their time and generosity in answering my endless questions. I used the collections of the State Library of Victoria to read diaries and accounts of young women and lighthouse keepers from the era, and the National Library of Australia's excellent resource, Trove, to examine newspaper articles, including the records of the inquest into Harriet Parker's death.

The historical records of the Cape St George Lighthouse make no mention of Aboriginal people, evidence of the way in which the historical record so often ignores the ongoing colonisation and dispossession of the traditional custodians of this land. The stories and experiences of Aboriginal people are not mine to tell but are ones that I respectfully acknowledge.

The context and depiction of the Aboriginal characters in this work has been influenced by my research into the Gurnai Kurnai people during the nineteenth century, in the area now known as East Gippsland.

A number of resources were useful as I approached this aspect of the book, and I am grateful for the Australia Council's *Protocols for Producing Indigenous Australian Writing* and the Australian Society of Author's *Writing About Indigenous Australia* resources, produced by Dr Anita Heiss and Terri Janke.

Kate Gibson and Harriet Parker became my Kate and Harriet. I have only guessed at what might have occurred between them, and I do not know what became of the real Kate. I hope that my imaginings do justice to the real lives these women led.